Praise for Skye Taylor

"Time to pack up and head to Florida where revenge makes for a bloody summer for Detective Jesse Quinn. Don't miss ***Bullseye***, a sensational kick-off to a fresh new mystery series." ~ C. Hope Clark, author of the award-winning Edisto Island Mysteries and The Carolina Slade Mysteries. www.chopeclark.com

"Since I live in St. Augustine, the settings in ***Bullseye*** were even more meaningful for me. But I also loved the twists and turns, the red herrings that threw us off track and the grit of the strong heroine, Jesse Quinn, who sometimes had to operate outside the rules to get the killer. I'm looking forward to the next in the series." ~ Kaye Schmitz, Amazon Reader

"Skye Taylor's ***Worry Stone*** is a deeply emotional tale. Authentic and evocative, this love story between a veteran and a one-time war protester makes us appreciate the healing power of love. I loved it!" ~ Eve Gaddy, National Bestselling author of Trouble in Texas

Falling for Zoe is a deftly plotted and delightful story of family, of real life, and love, and trying to do the right thing. ***Falling for Zoe*** is a romantic gem." ~ Cheryl Reavis, Best-selling, award-winning author

"Bravo Zulu for ***Healing a Hero***, filled with turmoil, tenderness, and painful secrets from the past. Will Gunnery Sergeant Philip Cameron have to choose between the Corps and the woman he loves?" ~ Heather Ashby, author of the Love in the Fleet series

~ CROSSFIRE ~

A talented graffiti artist has been vandalizing the Church of Peace, but there have been no leads. Then a bomb destroys half the church, and its pastor is found dead beneath the altar. The evidence is misleading, and Det. Jesse Quinn's tunnel-visioned partner is eager to arrest Jesse's next-door neighbor.

With her regular partner on family leave, Jesse is temporarily paired with her nemesis, a detective of the St John's County Sheriff's Office who thinks women don't belong on the Major Crimes squad. Zack Oliver is in a hurry to override her objections, close the case and move on. Jesse just needs to find the real killer of the popular local pastor before Zack pins the murder on an innocent man.

Meanwhile, at home, Jesse is trying to reconcile with her teenage daughter who is grounded for entertaining a boy in her bedroom. The teen is now lobbying to move into Jesse's ex's house where she thinks the rules will be more relaxed.

And then, there's Seth Cameron who would like to become more in Jesse's life than just a friend.

When did her life get so complicated?

The Jesse Quinn Mysteries
Bullseye
Crossfire

The Camerons of Tide's Way
Contemporary Romance
Falling for Zoe
Loving Meg
Trusting Will
Healing a Hero
Keeping His Promise
Worry Stone
Believing in Mac
Loving Ben (Short Story)
Mike's Wager (Short Story)

Time Travel Romance
Iain's Plaid

Political Intrigue
The Candidate

Dedication

To all those who serve in law enforcement, putting your lives on the line every day to deliver dangerous people to justice, all while juggling your own families and lives. Your commitment and sacrifices are appreciated, and I thank and honor all of you.

CROSSFIRE

A Jesse Quinn Mystery

Skye Taylor

SandCastleBooks

SandCastleBooks
ISBN: 978-1-7347431-7-3

Skye Taylor enjoys hearing from her readers.
Visit her at: www.Skye-writer.com

Cover design by Carrie Richter – The Monkey Factory

CHAPTER 1

STANDING AT PARADE REST in my dress uniform under a cloudless sky I did my best to ignore the trickles of sweat dampening the stiffly pressed fabric and to keep tears from unraveling my professional appearance. The boy next door was being buried way before his time.

My partner Rafe grimaced and jerked his head to indicate a radical church group crowded behind the barriers erected earlier by officers from the city of St. Augustine. The so-called Christians held banners with hate-filled taunts and chanted ugly refrains.

I was thankful for the overriding rumble of the idling motorcycles of the Patriot Riders. They'd added another layer of defense to the sheriff's department escort for the cortege both to the church and between the church and the cemetery.

A stiffening breeze caught a wayward strand of my hair and blew it across my face as a line of soldiers raised their rifles for the traditional three-volley gun salute. The echoes of the shots had barely faded away as the haunting sound of taps began. I ignored the tickling strands.

My phone vibrated in my pocket. I ignored it, as well. Today was Ryan's day.

Eight young men clad in dress uniforms from four branches of the military stepped forward, grasped the edges of the flag draped over Ryan's coffin and snapped it briskly upward, then began methodically

1

folding it into a precise triangle. My friend and neighbor, Natalie, pressed a gloved finger to her eye, brushing away a tear she probably suspected her son would not want her to shed. Ryan's dad Ty's face was rigid, doing his best to maintain his composure.

Natalie looked up as she accepted the neatly folded flag from the clean-shaven, dark skinned captain who presented it to her, a murmured thank you on her lips. Then the captain shook Ty's hand, executed an about face and marched back to his place.

My phone started rattling again.

Some kind of reception was to follow, and I had planned to attend, but the insistence of the incoming text wasn't to be ignored after all. I saw Rafe reach for his cell at the same moment.

We have an unattended death at 28 Hilltop. 17 y/o female on bed in bedroom. Patrol has the scene secured and crime scene techs enroute. I read the text twice, then glanced at Rafe. "I need to speak to the Andersons before I leave." So much for requesting the day off.

"Girl's not going anywhere," Rafe replied slipping his phone back into its holster. "A few more minutes won't matter to her."

As soon as the color guard and pall bearers marched away leaving the family in a small uncertain cluster, I hurried toward my grieving friends. I pulled Natalie into a tight hug. I wanted to say it was a beautiful send-off, or something similar, but it was a funeral. The funeral of a beloved son. Nothing beautiful in that. "I'm so sorry," was all I could muster. We rocked together mourning her baby boy for several long minutes. Then I reluctantly pulled away.

"I was planning to come back to the house, but I got called to work. I wish I didn't, but—"

"We understand." Ty cut me off with an extended hand. I ignored the hand and hugged the grieving dad, too.

I gave Ryan's brother and sisters a hug, then turned back to Natalie. "I'll stop by the house later."

She shooed me on my way with a gesture. Regretfully, I headed back to Rafe.

I'd ridden over with my partner figuring I'd bum a ride to the reception with someone headed that way, which seemed like a good thing now. He could drive while I spent the ride on my phone gathering more details about what we were walking into.

Broussard answered before my end of the call even rang. "How was the funeral?"

"Tough." I didn't need to say more. Our sergeant had seen more than his share of healthy young people buried before their time. He knew. "We're on our way to Hilltop now. Funeral was just ending when I got your text. How come you didn't send Zack or Tómas?" Since we'd been detailed for the funeral, it just seemed like another pair of detectives could have been dispatched to the scene of an unattended death.

"Everyone's already out. So, you're up. Really sorry, Jesse. Couldn't be helped. Get back to me as soon as you have more info." Broussard hung up before I could respond and ask what he knew that we didn't. Or *if* he knew anything we didn't.

I stared at my now silent phone feeling Rafe's gaze on me. "Anything we need to know?"

I shook my head. "Broussard was kind of abrupt. Didn't fill in any blanks. I hate it when kids die. This day just keeps getting worse."

Traffic was light on State Road 207 and all too soon we turned onto Hilltop, passing homes surrounded by old growth. Curving driveways with shrubbery mostly hid the modest homes from view, but it was clearly a neighborhood of families. The occasional basketball backboard here, a bike laid carelessly beside a drive there, a baby carriage being pushed along the winding sidewalk. Then came the cluster of patrol cruisers parked at odd angles, a shocking contrast to the quiet street up to this point. A rescue truck was backed into the driveway of the house we were headed for. Rafe managed to squeeze into a space across the street where an undeveloped lot offered a wide verge of unkempt grass before the trees began.

Unused to working in uniform, I debated leaving my cap in the car, but ended by plopping it onto my head. Better to be inconvenienced than half dressed.

As we hurried past the rescue truck, the crew was reloading their gear into the various doors it had come from. I caught the eye of a woman I recognized. She shook her head sadly. "Nothing we could do. She was gone long before we got here. Sad." The EMT went back to stowing gear.

"Cause?"

She shoved another gearbox into the truck before turning back. "Overdose be my guess."

I caught up to Rafe, and we stepped up onto the low brick porch together.

"Hey, Jesse. Rafe." My patrol friend, Rob McKenzie, greeted us, his handsome face drawn. "What's with the uniforms?"

"Just left a military funeral," I answered the young deputy. "I thought your beat was over on the east side. What are you doing way out here?"

"Filling in for a buddy. Wish I hadn't."

"What do you know? Did you go in?"

He nodded. "Another thing I wish I hadn't done. Just isn't right. Family name is Connors. Thirteen-year-old sister found her when she got home from school. Parents aren't home. Dead girl is Amy. She was gone when we got here. Sister is Lisa. Sue Cromwell is with the kid." Mac scowled at the end of his brief summary.

"Thanks. Catch you in a few," I said and stepped into the house with Rafe on my tail.

To my right, huddled on a brown tweed couch, in a comfortable, homey living room, sat a young girl with Sue Cromwell's arm wrapped around her heaving body. The deputy patted the girl's shoulder, caught my eye, and nodded toward a short hallway leading off the living room beyond the couch.

We followed the hallway toward the sound of voices and entered what was obviously a teenage girl's bedroom with posters of Taylor Swift and Harry Styles tacked up on the walls along with a collection of art featuring horses. A stack of books and folders spilled off a desk in one corner, a pile of dirty clothing filled another, and there was very little of the dark blue carpet showing beneath all the teenage clutter.

A third deputy and another EMT were just getting ready to leave as I pulled on the gloves I'd grabbed from Rafe's stash.

"Kabadi is on his way." The deputy said, referring to our M.E. "Pretty sure it's drugs, or perhaps drugs and alcohol mixed. We'll leave it to you." They edged past us and disappeared down the hall stripping off gloves and booties as they went.

Except for the pallor of her skin, Amy Connors might have been sleeping. I looked away, wishing I was anywhere but here. Wishing there was no need for Rafe and me to be in this girl's bedroom. Her parents would be devastated.

I forced myself to look at the girl on the bed and study the scene. Long pale blond hair spilled around Amy's pretty, youthful face. A sharp contrast against the ink blue pillowcase. Her arms splayed to the sides, palms up, defenseless and innocent. I swallowed the sense of loss that hit hard even though I'd never met her before. I said a silent prayer for her soul and for her parents and her sister who would, each in their own way, have to come to terms with what this girl may have done.

Then I gave myself a shake and got to work. With my phone, I began taking shots of the room and the girl. Rafe slid paper booties over his spit shined shoes before moving toward the piles of junk around the bed.

"Damn!" He straightened and held up a bright orange prescription bottle. He shook it, but there was no rattle. "Xanax. Why would a kid this young need Xanax?"

"Panic attacks. Depression." The depths of despair too often hidden even from those closest.

Rafe studied the bottle again before he dropped it into an evidence bag. "They weren't hers. Script's written for Emma Connors. Her mother, maybe?"

I looked at the girl, the empty glass on the nightstand, then back to the girl. The heavy sense of loss and futility tugged at my soul.

"That's going to add to the mother's guilt." With one last glance around the room, I decided to leave its exploration to Rafe. "I'm going to go talk to the kid sister."

I pulled the booties and gloves off at the door and retraced my steps back to the living room.

The girl on the couch hid behind a curtain of hair almost as pale as her sister's weeping softly while Deputy Cromwell tried to comfort her with soft murmurs of empathy. I slid onto the chair adjacent to the couch and reached out to curve my palm around one shuddering shoulder.

"Are you okay with answering a few questions?"

The girl shrugged without looking up.

"What's your name?"

"Lisa." Barely above a whisper.

"How old are you, Lisa?"

"Thirteen. I can't believe she really did it." Now she did look up, her ravaged face as tragic as the pale, placid one in the bedroom.

"Really did what, Lisa?" I leaned closer, withdrawing my hand and propping my elbows on my knees.

"She said she wanted to die. I didn't believe her. I thought she was just being Amy. You know, like, a drama queen."

"Do you know why she . . ." I couldn't bring myself to say kill herself to this fragile young girl. "Do you know what was bothering her?"

"Her boyfriend dumped her."

"Tell me about it." Might as well get the story while Amy's confession was still fresh in her sister's mind. Where were her parents, though? They should be here. "Where are your mom and dad?"

"They're at some dumb funeral. It isn't even anyone they knew. Just some guy who got killed fighting a war."

My mind flashed back to the chanting mob behind the barriers at Ryan Anderson's burial service. If that was the funeral Amy and Lisa's parents had attended, they were going to come home and find out firsthand what it felt like to lose a child. Maybe that would convince them to give up picketing soldier funerals. I would have a hard time being as sympathetic as I should be.

"Can you tell me what happened this afternoon?" I asked, returning to my initial line of questioning.

Lisa's swollen red eyes began to tear up again. "Amy didn't go to school today. She told Mom and Dad she was sick. And then . . . then

. . ." She hiccoughed and wept again in earnest. "W-when I got home, I found her like that. She wasn't breathing and she was cold." Lisa shuddered and tears ran down her cheeks in rivers. "I called 911. But it didn't help." The last word was a screech.

Deputy Cromwell gave me the evil eye and went back to soothing the crying girl. She was right. I could talk to the girl later about the boyfriend who dumped her sister and where she got the pills. But I suspected I already knew about those. It was too much of a coincidence for Emma Connors not to be Amy and Lisa Connors' mother. Or possibly a grandmother.

Rafe appeared in the doorway holding up an empty glass liquor flask.

CHAPTER 2

THE STREETLIGHTS HAD COME ON, casting a welcoming glow over our neighborhood by the time I pulled into my driveway. Exhaustion tugged at every bone in my body, and I ached to just shuck the uniform and collapse on my little deck with a glass of something with a little kick. But my day wasn't over.

My heart lifted a bit when I spied Seth Cameron's red Dodge Ram perched all alone on the edge of our short sandy road across from the Anderson's. He'd probably squeezed in between a cluster of other vehicles when he arrived, but they'd all departed since. Seth taught at the school where Ty worked and had tutored my son when Mike's failing grades had almost gotten him expelled. Seth was also the man I'd finally agreed to go out with recently. My first and only foray into dating since my divorce.

The Anderson house was ablaze with lights, which I'd expected. Mine was completely dark, which meant I had no idea where either of my kids were, unless they, like Seth, were still next door at the Anderson's.

That very long, very hot shower, my jammies and a tumbler of Glenfiddich would have to wait. I'd promised Natalie and Ty I'd stop by later and later had arrived.

I left my weapon secured in the trunk and headed next door across a well-kept lawn that must have been mowed earlier today given the lingering scent of freshly cut grass. No one answered my knock, but the inside door stood open, so I slid the screen aside and stepped inside.

My sixteen-year-old son sprawled on the couch watching *Paw Patrol* on the television with two curly-headed moppets tucked against his sides: the Anderson's oldest son's kids. I smiled at Mike, and he gave me a thumbs up, then went back to watching a show he'd never spend time on at home.

Natalie appeared with a pizza box balanced on one hand and a clutch of paper plates and napkins in the other. She plopped it all on the coffee table, and all three boys surged forward to grab a slice. She noticed me over the tops of their heads. "I didn't hear you come in. Sorry."

I crossed the room and enveloped her in a hug. "Don't be. How are you all managing?"

She gave me a weary smile. "Mike is a treasure. You should be proud how patient he's been with those two rascals. They miss Ryan, I guess, but I don't think they really understand that he's gone for good this time. Mike took them to the beach and wore them out for us." A pause. "Don't know how I'd have gotten through this week without your family, Jesse."

Pride swelled in my chest. It's nice when someone else confirms you raised your kid right. "Is Jacqui around?"

"She left . . ." Natalie frowned for a moment. "Around three, I think. Your mom stopped in, and Jacqui left with her. Jacqui helped with the luncheon. Such a nice young lady she's growing up to be."

Good. I could relax and just be Natalie's friend for a bit. I repeated my earlier question. "How are *you* doing? Where is everyone?"

Natalie nodded toward the kitchen and sagged onto a wooden bench by the door. One, if I remembered correctly, Ryan had made for her. I joined her.

"I feel like I've cried an ocean dry." Yet her eyes grew watery with more tears even before the words were said. Clearly, she hadn't cried herself out. Not yet. Maybe not ever.

Emma and Lou Conners edged into my mind. In a few days, they too, would be burying a precious child. How did one cope with such a loss? Kids are supposed to bury their parents, not the other way around.

"Nat? You okay?" A deep voice cut into my melancholy thoughts. Ty strode over, squatted, and gave his wife a long, deep hug, then twisted toward me.

We both stood and I wrapped my arms around his middle. He returned the embrace. "I'm so sorry, Ty. I just don't have words to tell you how much." I pulled back and looked up into his coffee brown face. A face creased with loss and pain. "Is there anything I can do?"

I'd asked this question a dozen times since two officers had arrived on their doorstep more than a week past. The answer was always the same. *Can't think of anything.*

Ty dropped his arms. "C'mon out to the kitchen. We've got more adult options in food and beverage out there."

Mike and his charges were focused on pizza and the big screen TV, so I let Ty lead the way to the kitchen where Seth who was plucking a shrimp from a platter and popping it into his mouth, looked up and winked at me.

"How come you didn't tell me you were dating that wonderful man?" Natalie hissed in my ear.

I whispered back over my shoulder. "We aren't. Officially." One date didn't mean Seth and I were *dating*. Did it? A flush began to warm my cheeks.

Just before the Andersons had received the news about Ryan, I'd gotten more dressed up than I'd been in years and Seth had taken me to *The Columbia* for an elegant dinner. A date he'd conned me into after delivering flowers to my office along with the claim that the glorious arrangement celebrated the sixth month anniversary of the day his life had changed. That change being the day we'd met in the principal's office at my son's school. It was a declaration that surprised me, but maybe shouldn't have.

Six months previously, Mike had been close to failing and repeating a year due to acting out over his father's defection, our subsequent divorce, and anger over the way Elliott had treated me. With Seth's help, Mike regained his straight-A status, did some serious growing up and was again on speaking terms with his father. Seth had also helped Mike rebuild the Camaro that Mike would soon be driving.

I'd spent the same six months trying to convince myself the instant attraction I'd felt to the ex-Navy-pilot-turned-teacher would pass, and it wasn't a good time for me to get emotionally involved with another man. It was a struggle enough to keep up with my very consuming job and single motherhood. Besides, I wasn't sure I had the energy for another relationship. So I'd kept Seth at arm's length despite his obvious interest in me. Putting my heart out there again after being blindsided by Elliott's betrayal, was a risk I was afraid to take.

Natalie bumped shoulders with me. "Give the guy a break. He's a keeper."

An echoed refrain. My partner, Rafe, had said something similar.

The chatter in the kitchen gave me respite from having to reply. Ryan's older brother Chase hurried toward me for a hug and his wife waved, her mouth full. Kiara, the older of two sisters in the Anderson family, just out of college and currently working in New York City, waved a gloved hand at me, then went back to scrubbing something in the sink, hiding her beautiful brown eyes, still heavy with tears.

Seth smiled, and my heart did a somersault. Who was I kidding? My heart was already involved whether I wanted it to be or not. I'd spent the entire evening at *The Columbia* entranced by that smile and feeling a tad breathless.

"Hey, Seth," I said, doing my best to keep that breathless quality out of my voice. "You didn't have to hang out here 'till I got back."

Seth's glance flitted to Ty, then back to me. "Well," he drawled in that distinctive North Carolina accent that I found so charming. "I asked for the whole day off. Where else would I be?"

Seth and Ty were friends. He was here for Ty. The flush in my cheeks heated up. "Okay. Now I'm really embarrassed," I replied, owning my self-centered assumption.

Seth speared another shrimp, dipped it in a bowl of dressing and held it in my direction. "Try one. The lady that brought them said the sauce was a secret recipe. I might have to kidnap her kid and hold him hostage for it."

Ty speared another dripping shrimp, tucked it into his mouth and nodded in agreement.

Natalie left us and crossed to the window overlooking her back yard, gazing out to the guest house that had been turned into an apartment for Ryan when he wasn't deployed somewhere else in the world. Not that Ryan had spent a lot of time there given he was away more than he was home, but it had been his place. And he'd never be coming back there again. Never striding across the lawn to claim a cup of early morning coffee with his parents. I joined her at the window. "I can't imagine how awful all this is for you and Ty."

A tear slipped down Natalie's cheek. "I think I'm still numb. Like maybe next week it will really hit me. Especially when we have to go through his things and clear the place out."

I tucked a wayward curl behind her ear. "Take your time. Let yourself grieve. There's no deadline."

She sighed. "Actually, there is. Ty's dad needs a place to go. His Alzheimer's is at the point where he can't live alone. We've had him on a waiting list for almost six months. They called this morning to say a room would become available next week. Did we still want it?"

"And you said . . .?" How did Ty's dad and Ryan's cottage tie together?

"Ty wants to bring him here. Let him live in—" Natalie swallowed hard. "In Ryan's place."

I glanced back at Ty as a wave of protective rebellion rolled through me. "And Ty told them no?" He should have consulted Natalie first.

Natalie shook her head. "He told them he'd call them tomorrow. That we were burying our son today and couldn't discuss it."

I began to understand the rush. The assisted living facility wouldn't hold the room long and Ty's dad needed some kind of permanence. Not shuffled off to the center and then here if they changed their mind or the other way around.

"He really should come here," Natalie said turning away from the window. "He loves to fish, and he'd be close. Closer than over on Route 1. He wouldn't be surrounded by strangers, but he'd still have someone watching out for him. I just—" She bit her top lip. "I just wish I didn't have to go through Ryan's stuff so soon. If it weren't for Papa Leroy needing to move in, I might never go through it at all. Just lock the door and never go back there again."

"I could help—"

Natalie jerked her head stiffly. "I need . . . I need to do it by myself."

I wrapped an arm about her waist and gave her a squeeze. "Well, you know where to find me if you change your mind."

"Tell me about your day," Natalie said, squeezing back and changing the subject.

My heart thudded, suddenly drowning in anguish. I shook my head. Hearing about another dead child was the last thing Natalie needed. And the last thing I wanted to discuss. Tomorrow would be soon enough to dig into the unhappy loss of a pretty, young girl with so much to live for.

CHAPTER 3

AFTER WE LEFT THE ANDERSONS to their quiet and grief, Seth walked me across the lawn, one hand resting lightly against the small of my back. The glow of a nearly full moon lit our way, and a soft breeze played through the curls that had finally escaped my braid to tickle my face and neck. He stopped at the foot of the stairs and turned me to face him.

"You look beat, so I won't ask to come up. Tomorrow won't be any easier if you don't get some sleep." He kissed me briefly on the mouth, then touched a thumb to the place his lips had just been. "Night, Jess."

Something in me wanted to call out to him as he started across the street to his truck, wanted to call him back and suggest . . . suggest what exactly? I wasn't into begging. And didn't even know just what it was I wanted. *Maybe you just don't want to be alone*, my inner self suggested as I watched the broad shoulders and dark hair melt into the night. The stride and shape of him had become so familiar and his company so welcome.

The truck's interior light came on, he climbed in, then blew me another kiss and shut the door. I stayed where I was until his taillights disappeared, then sighed and mounted the stairs to my home.

Mike had already returned and gone to his room and the house was as quiet as it ever gets with the ocean practically in our back yard. I changed out of my uniform and hung it up, even though it needed cleaning after wearing it all day. Then I wandered through the empty rooms, unable to settle, wishing Seth had offered to come in, or I'd had the chutzpah to ask. That innocent young girl, lying so still and beyond help, remained in my head. I could have done without the echoes of the sister sobbing. Or the shock on their parents' faces.

I considered calling Rafe to talk strategy for the morning, but turned the television on instead, found an old movie and finally poured that tumbler of Glenfiddich.

The ice in the scotch had melted and the television was broadcasting infomercials when I woke just as dawn began to cast faint shadows across the living room carpet. *Getting old is a bitch*, I thought as I sat up, creaking and stiff. There was a time I could sleep comfortably anywhere, especially on my couch. But it was more than age this morning. The anguish of two young souls snuffed way too soon hung about me like a shroud.

I pulled my sneakers on and headed out for a run to banish the cobwebs. The beach was best this early in the day with the rising sun painting the sky fantastic colors and no one else in sight. By the time I pulled to a stop out front and began my cool-down stretches, the stiffness of sleeping on the couch was gone. Two large mugs of very black coffee later and my brain was in gear. A scalding shower finished the job.

Now, here I was in the antiseptic atmosphere of the county morgue, clad in paper booties, gown and mask, attending to my least favorite part of being a detective.

I scratched at an itch on my cheek, paper gown crinkling. Dr. Kabati, medical examiner for St John's County, spoke into the mike as he proceeded with the autopsy on the presumed suicide of seventeen-year-old Amy Conners.

Watching Sandeep cut, sadness crept back in, leaving a chill even another hot shower wouldn't have been able to shake. What could have been so unbearable that this beautiful young woman should take her own life? Presumed . . . we still hadn't found any notes left behind saying goodbye to her parents or her sister. There had been no sign of foul play. Just the sleeping beauty on the bed without a pulse, a prescription bottle in the waste basket without any pills, an empty glass on the nightstand and a vodka flask with nothing left inside on the floor under the bed.

Both parents' fingerprints had been lifted from the pill bottle, but there were logical reasons why they should be there, and both parents had been horrified when they came home to the news. The vodka glass had been clean except for Amy's prints and those on the vodka flask likely belonged to an adult in the house as well, unless she'd found someone willing to sell to a minor. Sandeep's estimated time of death gave all three family members an alibi.

I wasn't even sure where to hunt for other possibilities. Amy's sister hadn't known who the boyfriend was, which I thought odd. Maybe not so much for her parents. Some teens are pretty closed mouth when it comes to sharing things with their mother and father, but her sister? They attended the same school. They were only a few years apart in age. Sisters shared stuff like that, didn't they?

If the boyfriend was a fellow student, his attendance at school would rule him out for complicity, but a kid who dumped a girl wasn't much of a suspect in the first place. Rafe was pursuing a search warrant to go through Amy's phone and computer. Maybe something would turn up to put this case to bed.

Sandeep stepped back from the table, nodded to his assistant, then turned to me. "Any questions I haven't covered?"

I shook my head. "I know where to find you if anything new comes up." Then taking one last glance at the remains on the table. I headed for the door.

The Connors' living room looked as though a cleaning crew had come through in the night leaving everything showroom fresh. Emma Connors probably hadn't even gone to bed or tried to sleep and buried her grief in busyness. She'd already gone out when Rafe and I arrived.

Rafe interviewed Amy's dad in the garage. I joined Lisa on the couch where she'd been yesterday. Maybe she'd never left it.

"Are you sure you don't know who your sister's boyfriend was?" I prodded the grieving girl as gently as I could.

Lisa's eyes were red and puffy, but she'd stopped crying. For now, at least. "She wouldn't tell me, and he wasn't from our school."

"But she told you she was upset about the breakup. What exactly did she say about it?"

"Just that he dumped her for someone else. But—" She pinched her lips and sniffled.

"But?" I prompted.

"Amy acted like the breakup was all her fault. She—I don't know exactly how to put it." Lisa closed her eyes as if seeking an explanation inside her eyelids. "She was embarrassed." Eyes open again, Lisa shrugged. "And maybe a little guilty? That doesn't make much sense, I know. Amy was smart. I mean, like really smart. But she was awful dumb about boys."

I patted her hands where they lay writhing in her lap. "Thank you for speaking with me again. I know this is difficult, and I appreciate your help."

Rafe appeared in my peripheral vision.

Tight-lipped, he jerked his head toward the door. He had a laptop clutched against his chest and a smart phone in one hand. Amy's mother was at the funeral home and there was nothing more to be learned here.

With one last glance back at the wilting girl on the couch, I followed Rafe to the door.

"Anything helpful?" I asked as soon as he backed out of the driveway.

"Nada. Dad had very little knowledge of his daughter's current friends, activities or even her mood of late. We need to talk to her mother."

"I know where she is. Maybe we can catch her before she leaves?"

Rafe tilted his head. "Point me in the right direction."

"Brooks Funeral Parlor," I said, just as my phone buzzed.

I answered, listened to Sandeep's report, thanked him, and hung up. "Cause of death, overdose mixed with alcohol. Nothing we didn't already know. Highly unlikely anyone helped her, but let's talk to her mother before we close the file."

Mrs. Connors was unlocking her car door as we pulled into Brooks' parking lot. Rafe pulled up next to the minivan.

"Mrs. Connors," I said getting out. "We'd like to ask a few questions. Can we buy you a cup of coffee at City Perk?"

Swollen but currently dry, Emma Connors' eyes gazed back at me with the empty look of grief. She rubbed at her chest and replied in a flat tone. "I guess."

"Thank you. I know this is a difficult time and we appreciate it. We'll meet you there so you'll have your car when we're done," I replied, stepping back to allow her access to her car.

The mid-morning rush was over and the only sound in the popular coffee shop was the clink of crockery mugs being stacked in a dishwasher somewhere out of sight. The heavy scent of coffee was a welcome change-up from either the autopsy room or the polish scented living room at the Connors' home. And I was enjoying my third cup of joe for the day.

With her hands wrapped tightly around her warm mug, Emma Connors gazed past us, seeming to see nothing. "She never talked about boys. Not about dating them, anyway. She was Mensa you know. She spent all her time with her nose buried in books." The woman finally brought her gaze back to me. "Ever heard about the AICE program? It's an international certification course. Very demanding. Only smart kids get into it and even smart kids have to work hard to succeed. Amy wanted to go to Cambridge University when she graduated. I can't believe she did this." Tears brimmed over again, and we waited while the woman mopped her eyes and pulled herself together.

I had heard about the program. Students were required to do community service and some of them had volunteered at the Sheriff's office. Maybe Amy Connors had met her young man outside of school while her parents thought she was involved in whatever outside project she'd chosen. I posed the question.

Mrs. Connors jerked back. "Amy would never ignore her responsibilities. She was as diligent in her work at St. Francis House as she was in her studies."

"So, St. Francis House was where she was doing her community service?"

Amy's mother nodded. "She helped with meals. Once a week. Sometimes twice if another group couldn't make their regular night."

"Do you know all the students in her group?"

"Amy didn't have any boyfriends. Not that she brought home to meet us, anyway. Besides, if Amy was involved with a boy, it wasn't there. There were only girls in that group. She never confided in us…" Mrs. Connors broke off with a whimper.

Clearly, we were not going to learn anything new.

Before we closed the case, though, we'd hack into the girl's computer. She was a loner, brilliant and probably awkward, most likely swept off her feet by some eager young man, then dumped and shattered.

Rafe left a bill on the table and stood. I thanked Mrs. Connors, offered my sympathies again and joined him.

"If there's anything we can do for you or your family, just call. Dr. Kabadi will be releasing your daughter's body perhaps as early as tomorrow so you can get on with your plans." I pushed my card across the table. "My cell number's on the back."

We left the woman still clinging to her now cold mug. With a twinge of guilt, I yearned for home and my troublesome daughter to hug and tell her how much I loved her, to assure her how proud I was of her and that I'd always be there for her.

Back at central, Rafe and I ran into our lieutenant's minion as soon as we stepped into the building.

"The Lieutenant wants to see you ASAP." Dalton snickered, then swaggered back down the hall, pleased with himself.

I gritted my teeth against stronger language. "Might as well get it over with. Whatever *it* is."

Rafe pointed toward the door to the men's room. "Lemme hit the head first."

I leaned against the wall checking my phone for texts from Lt.

Ward I might have missed and hence not answered, which would have triggered Dalton's being sent to grab us as soon as we showed up. Nope. Nothing.

Rafe reappeared and we headed toward Ward's office.

I tapped on the lieutenant's doorframe when we found neither Dalton nor the clerk usually on stationed outside.

"Come." Ward's voice didn't sound either angry or impatient. Good sign?

The Lieutenant gestured to two chairs opposite his desk.

"Any surprises on the Connors girl?"

"Nothing. Heartbreaking, but clearly self-inflicted. We'll have the closed file on your desk before the end of the day," I promised.

Ward sat back in his chair and fiddled with the pen he'd been writing with. "The file can wait. I have something else for you."

Rafe's expression mirrored my own. Lieutenant Ward was all about tying up loose ends and closing cases as quickly as possible.

"I'd like you to talk to Deputy Acosta. I know this isn't your usual area of investigation, but Acosta's new to the division and he could use a little help."

Paul Acosta worked burglary, break-ins, vandalism, and property crimes. Definitely not a crime we usually got tasked to investigate.

"What's up?" Rafe asked.

"Church of Peace has repeatedly reported graffiti on their buildings. No thefts or break-ins, just the obscene graffiti. As soon as they clean it up, something else appears. Acosta has no leads. Just give his work a look-over and see if anything jumps out at you." Ward sat forward and pulled a closed file off an imposing pile on the far corner of his desk. A clear dismissal.

As we walked back to our own tiny cubicle, Rafe pulled out his phone and initiated a call. "Hey, Paul. Ward said you wanted to meet with us." He hesitated a minute. "Yeah. Now's good. Is there any coffee in the pot over there? See you in a few."

Rafe pointed in the other direction. "He'll meet us in the conference room."

"Can't believe we've been demoted to graffiti."

"Or promoted to instructor," Rafe said, always with the positive, glass half full, attitude.

"Obscenities, huh?" I muttered, adjusting my own attitude. "Bet I could come up with something appropriately offensive to paint on that pissant's walls after he and his chanting disciples crashed Ryan's funeral. Ty Anderson's shock and Natalie's tears are stuck in my head, and I don't think they'll ever forget the disrespect hurled at their dead son."

CHAPTER 4

DEPUTY ACOSTA STRODE INTO THE ROOM with far more confidence than I'd expected. Younger by at least ten years he'd come up through the ranks quickly. Maybe he had reason for the self-confidence despite spinning his wheels on the Church of Peace graffiti case. He was handsome enough to get a gig modeling for GQ yet he'd chosen law enforcement. With streaks of sunlight in his wavy brown hair and a taut athletic body, he appeared comfortable in his skin, and aware of all his virtues.

He dropped a file onto the conference room table and flipped it open to reveal an 8 x 10 photo in full color. I gasped.

Like a gory accident you just can't look away from, my gaze stayed glued to the obscenity.

An enormous depiction of a human penis, along with equally impressive testicles, detailed right down to the genital hair sprouting from the sac. The whole loomed over the tall arched windows at the front of the Church of Peace.

"Jayyyyzus!" Rafe drawled.

The artist was quite talented, if misguided.

Rafe glanced at me before pushing it aside to reveal the next photo in the file. "Are they all this graphic?"

"Just that one. The others have a different feel to them." Paul spread out a series of photos.

Same wall. Same arched windows, but in one picture the black symbol for woman with a fist in the center representing the "My Body,

My Choice" movement. Another photo showed the windows covered with words—the kind of words one uses to describe a dirty old man.

Rafe put a finger on the corner of one photo and turned it. A silhouette of a woman kneeling, hair shrouding her face as if she was weeping. This one was different than the others, most of which had some sort of sexual overtones even without the outright obscenity of the first one he'd showed us.

On a completely different topic, the last image was of artwork that included an American Flag surrounded by half a dozen Patriot Riders astride their hogs facing off against Price himself. Pretty accurate rendition of Price the last time I'd seen him at Ryan's funeral.

"Would have been nice if the artist signed his work," Rafe muttered pushing the images into fan.

"How long has this been going on?"

"Couple of months." Paul tapped the "My Body, My Choice" symbol. "This is the oldest one. Appeared right after his lot picketed that abortion clinic down in Palm Coast. Weeping girl right after that. Then a two-week break. I hoped whoever had done it, had vented their anger, and moved on. But then the penis showed up followed by the nasty name-calling."

"Think they're aimed at the pastor?" I asked, pulling out my notebook. I had my own reasons to hate the man, but they had to do with picketing Ryan's funeral, not anything sexual. I pulled the Patriot Riders from the pile and studied it again. This one was surely meant to get back at the pastor and those of his flock that I'd personally experienced so recently.

Paul lifted one shoulder. "Everyone I interviewed speaks as if Winston Price is the second coming. Nothing but praise. *Such a dear man. So humble. Giving. Caring. And the most eligible bachelor in town.*" Paul mimicked an admiring feminine tone, but I got the impression he didn't believe it. "He's raised a ton of money. There is that impressive sanctuary he and everyone who attends Church of Peace is so proud of, and he's created a couple trusts that hand out money to several legitimate charities. He's personally involved in the meals that are put on at St Francis House for the homeless, organizing food drives and volunteers." That was the second time that day I'd heard a reference to St. Francis House and my ears perked up.

"He's young, good-looking and energetic," Paul continued. "And did I mention wealthy? The older ladies in his parish think he walks on water, and I'd guess there were quite a few young women who would be eager to strike up a closer relationship. But no one said anything that explains these." Paul tapped the pile of photos. "Not even the men I ran down."

Fletcher Ward, not my immediate boss, but a lieutenant heavy on micro-managing the department, must really hate me. I thought we'd come to a truce over my flaunting his orders last month. But apparently not. Not if he was sticking me with solving Pastor Price's public relations problems.

Paul answered a question that hadn't been asked. "Whoever is doing this has been very careful about not leaving behind any clues. No footprints. No tire tracks. No fingerprints. Nothing. Except the extraordinary artwork. Got to admire that, at least. Whoever is doing it could make a living selling paintings downtown at the Plaza. Look at this one."

Paul shuffled through the stack again and slapped another large image on the table. This one a black and white depicting an infant in the womb. Softer and more compelling than an ultrasound, as if a camera had been inserted into the mother's womb. The infant sucked its thumb and even had a dimple in its cheek. Slashing viciously across the beautiful image, however, was a band of solid black.

I swallowed hard. While I championed individual rights, I was adamantly anti-abortion. The image made me cringe. But settling that issue was not my job. "What do you think the artist was saying? Are they for or against abortion?"

"Price and his faithful following picket abortion clinics, which suggests whoever painted this was pro-choice." Paul shook his head, a pained look crossing his handsome features. "But the care taken with this drawing seems to say something very different." He shook his head again.

I tore my gaze away from the image of a preborn child. "What does

Price have to say?"

"He wants whoever it is to be caught and stopped, but he's a turn-the-other-cheek kind of guy. Doesn't want to prosecute. Insists it's God's place to judge the actions, not man's."

"So, we're wasting our time chasing down the perp," Rafe summed it up.

A total waste of deputy hours and taxpayer dollars. I *tsked*, thought briefly of my mother's disapproval, and *tsked* again. The church was private property and if the pastor refused to press charges nothing would be done. Even if we could catch the guy. Or woman.

"Why does he even bother to call us in if he doesn't want to prosecute?" A headache was beginning to take shape and I bit back a cuss.

Paul grimaced. "Like I said, he wants it stopped. Not prosecuted. He—" The young deputy grabbed for his phone, glanced at it and raised one finger with an apologetic look, then brought it to his ear. "Reverend!" Paul mouthed the words, *Speak of the devil.* He listened, closing his eyes with a pinched furrow between his brows. "Yes, sir. About twenty minutes. See you shortly."

He jabbed angrily at the phone and shoved it into the holster on his belt. "Here we go again. You guys want to take a ride?"

True to Paul's word, twenty minutes later we pulled into the church parking lot. Rafe and I followed Paul, neither of us had any desire to sit behind the grate in the back seat of Paul's department issued vehicle.

I slid out from behind Rafe's mounted laptop and gazed up at the impressive edifice. I'd seen it before, but still the grandeur overwhelmed me. The front of the church rose like the prow of an ocean liner overhanging thousands of panes of glass with light twinkling through from dozens of crystal chandeliers within. The whole façade was guarded by a row of impressive columns built of the same stone as the church itself.

The newest assault in hues of brown and gold depicted a soldier's rifle upended in a pair of combat boots with a helmet perched on top. An image to honor a dead hero. Another impressive display of talent.

An incredible feat of daring because this time the graffiti covered most of that ostentatious expanse of glass, clearly visible from the street where anyone driving by could have seen the image coming to life. The lower panes of glass were whited out and the words, *May God mete out justice to those who spit on soldiers' graves* was written in bold red cursive. It must have taken hours.

"Unfucking believable!" Rafe muttered.

"Definitely wanted to make a statement," I agreed. A statement I had to agree with.

"That's a change-up." Paul's voice was as full of awe as my gut. "Guess he's been picketing funerals again."

"Two days ago. A kid named Ryan Anderson. Army in Afghanistan." Rafe filled him in. "We were there and saw Price and his minions. Thankfully they were kept at a distance due to the Patriot Riders, but they were there and obvious with their insults."

"Damn. I read about that Ryan fellow. Wasn't he the EOD tech supporting a squad of Special Forces?"

I nodded, then answered verbally as Paul's awed gaze stayed fixed on the graffiti.

Paul finally tore his gaze away from the building and looked at Rafe. "Someone you knew?"

Rafe waved a thumb in my direction. "His parents are her neighbors. We attended the funeral representing the Sheriff."

I thought of my friends and wished I could reward the artist. A brief image of Natalie perched on a stool, painting beautifully detailed landscapes flitted through my head. But she wouldn't have done this. Never mind it would have required ladders and hours of time, she had an in-law apartment to clean out and a father-in-law with Alzheimer's to get settled. Still, I couldn't help myself. "The good pastor sure deserved it this time."

Paul started walking toward the side of the building. "Might as well take the bastard's report. I hope you can stomach the arrogant prick and his puffed-up outrage."

Rafe and I jerked into action and followed Paul along an elaborately bricked path that led around neatly trimmed shrubbery to the side of the church. Paul stopped when we reached a portico high enough to allow a school bus to pass underneath to discharge passengers right at the church door and glanced up.

"They only took half my advice." Paul pointed to motion activated cameras mounted to capture any activity on this side of the building. "I told them to mount cameras to monitor all sides. Not sure why Price would cut corners and leave the main canvas unguarded."

I retreated to the front of the building again, but Paul was right. Not a single camera had been mounted anywhere to keep an eye on the impressive prow of the sanctuary. I returned to the men. "All that glass. What an invitation to someone throwing rocks."

"But who is without sin?" muttered Rafe, quoting from John's gospel.

"Price thinks he is," Paul said, pulling open a massive mahogany door.

We stepped into the cool interior and found ourselves in a vestibule. Several pieces of leather upholstered furniture sat in small groupings around dark wood tables graced with large ornate lamps. A scattering of religious pamphlets lay on the tables and an Oriental rug covered a good portion of the tiled floor.

A beaming woman sailed toward us from the far side of the room. "May I help you?" An open door behind her revealed what looked like the church offices, brightly lit, with the corner of a desk showing and a wall of file cabinets beyond.

"Oh, it's you, Deputy Acosta." The woman pressed her lips together and shook her head. "I don't know what the world is coming to when people can defile a house of God. This way, please." She turned and headed back the way she'd come, and we followed like baby ducklings in her wake. At a door marked *Reverend Winston Price* in gold leaf, she turned. "Pastor Price has been waiting for you, and he's not pleased."

CHAPTER 5

WINSTON PRICE SURGED TO HIS FEET and planted his hands on his desk. "When are you going to put a stop to this outrage?"

"I'm working on it, Pastor Price," Acosta replied with diplomatic calm.

My hackles rose. *When you stop insulting everyone who disagrees with you,* I wanted to say.

We hadn't been asked to take a seat, so of course, that's what I did. Rafe copied me, then Paul.

Price remained standing, huffing like an overweight runner after an up-hill sprint. "This has been going on for weeks and you haven't done a thing."

"There has been little to go on and even if we had found the culprit, you've made it clear you don't wish to prosecute," Paul said evenly. Acosta was going places in the world of law enforcement politics . . . a lot farther than I ever would.

And you're wasting our time. Time better spent on people we could help. I pulled out my phone and turned on the record feature. Rafe just folded his hands in his lap.

I took a moment to study my surroundings. As impressive as the church itself. Ceilings higher than usual in any office, even here in the south where fans were employed to move air away from those below. Floor to ceiling bookcases covered the wall behind the pastor's desk filled with leather bound volumes that didn't look like they'd ever been opened. The adjacent wall was of glass and looked out to the wooded area behind the church. That expanse of grass interrupted by a small gazebo. Perhaps used for photo shoots of weddings and the like.

The floor was covered with another massive Oriental carpet and all the chairs were upholstered in leather. The desk itself was another display of power and wealth, all polished wood, probably cherry given the dark expensive look of it.

"Why don't you sit down and tell us what you know about this latest . . . instance," Paul suggested, dragging my attention back to the matter at hand.

Price glowered for another long moment, then dropped into his seat. He'd be handsome if he wasn't scarlet faced, nostrils flaring. With dark hair, deep blue eyes, and a fashionable scruff, he must turn quite a few feminine heads. That, along with his wealth. I'd seen his multi-million-dollar home. He'd be considered quite a catch. If you could put up with his politics. And his ego.

"I called dispatch first thing when I came in this morning," Price began in a strident tone. "That . . . that offensive painting was not there when I left after Sunday services. Mondays the church offices are closed, and no one is here. Clearly this was done yesterday. And it's—" He broke off and stretched an arm out to reveal a Cartier watch that probably cost more than I made in a month. "It's nearly three in the afternoon. What took you so long?"

Time to butt in and set a new pace. "What time did you leave on Sunday?" And how was it that not a single person in his congregation hadn't noticed the image and seen fit to apprise him of it before now?

Price turned to me, a look of distaste marring his features. Maybe he didn't like female cops. Or women in general. Fine with me. Those were the easiest to fluster.

"It's possible the job was started on Sunday," I suggested.

"Sacrilege," the irate man spat.

"What time?" I prodded.

"Who would paint something so offensive?" Price asked, ignoring my question again.

Two military funerals were disrupted by Price and his disciples in just one week. One of Ryan Anderson's fellow soldiers, caught in the same ambush, was buried Friday at the National Cemetery in Jacksonville. Then Ryan here in St Augustine on Saturday. Payback?

Rafe finally stuck an oar in the water. "Did you leave directly after services on Sunday?"

"Yes. No." Price shook his head. "I mean, pretty much. I spoke to a few people after the service, but then locked up and went home."

His only Sunday service ended at twelve, but I wanted to force him to answer my question. "And what time would that have been?"

Price sat back, his color fading, apparently unable to keep the extreme ire going. "One. Maybe one-thirty."

"And you did not return to the building again until today?"

"No."

"You didn't drive past it at any time in between?"

"No."

"Not even to admire the sun setting against those magnificent windows?" I needled.

He only grunted, missing my intended slur.

"And no one in your congregation noticed it either, I'm assuming." Price glared at me.

Time for another angle of attack. "Has anyone made threats?"

"Threats?" Price sounded shocked.

"To your face, or by phone. Perhaps left threatening messages on your answering machine?"

"I do not know why anyone would wish to make threats against a man of God," Price blustered.

"Someone hated you or what you stand for enough to spend hours painting the message we saw on our way in." To say nothing of the amount of paint and talent.

Rafe launched into another round of questions about parishioners with a beef, perhaps neighbors of the church building itself who resented the crowded, noisy Sundays. To all of which Price had no answers.

I'd had about all I could stomach of the man, so I stood, pulled a card from my pocket, and pushed it across the polished desk. "We'll let you know what we learn, when we learn it."

Paul and Rafe shot to their feet, apparently as eager to be gone as I was. We filed out with Price firing veiled threats about ineffective deputies and one-sided law enforcement at our backs.

Rafe gave me a wry grin outside. "So much for Christian sympathy and forbearance."

"I sure hope Ward doesn't expect us to spend hours chasing this case down," I said as we left the building. "Guy deserves every bit of the harassment."

"But it's his parishioners who get to clean up the mess," Paul said. "Even if they don't always agree with him."

"Then they should find another church."

"They've been brainwashed," Rafe offered, gesturing to the grand façade with its equally grand graffiti. "Only answer to how he managed to get them to fork over enough dinero to build this place. You hand over your life savings, you are kind of compelled to stay, or swallow your pride and admit you were fleeced."

"The people I've interviewed definitely talk like they've drunk the Kool-Aid," Paul said.

I snorted. "Which probably rules out an irate parishioner. Might as well split up and speak to a few neighbors. Maybe someone saw something this time. Or saw something and is willing to admit it this time." I turned my back to the painted church front and studied the houses across the street. "I'll take those three houses." I gestured to three modest homes on the south side of the street that had the best view of the glass expanse of the church even if they wouldn't have seen anyone parked in the lot adjacent. "You guys try the places on either side going north. Maybe someone saw unusual activity in the parking lot on a day we are told no one would be here."

"I spoke to several neighbors after the phallic depiction appeared," Paul said. "Claimed not to see anything. Might have been the truth. Or maybe they thought Price deserved it and had no plans to rat anyone out."

I headed for the street. "Still, we've got to go through the motions or Price's threats will have teeth. Besides, this might have been a whole new bunch considering the change of topic."

"I think I'll move my ride first," Rafe said to my back.

"Good idea." I waved over my shoulder and continued toward the road.

Finding witnesses willing to help find the perpetrator might be difficult, but I'd give it the old college try so Ward couldn't find fault.

No one answered at the first house I came to, so I traipsed across a toy-strewn lawn to an identical, single-story home with an attached garage and a high fence behind it, possibly surrounding a pool. Or maybe, my snide mind suggested, to shut out the church across the street.

A harried looking young woman answered the door with a toddler clinging to one leg and a baby on the other hip. "Yes?"

"Deputy Jesse Quinn." I showed her my star and asked if I could come in to ask a few questions.

Her eyes flitted to the church for a fraction of a second. A telling second.

"Sure. Danny, please let go." She brushed the toddler off her leg and unlatched the screen.

The child stomped his chubby legs in protest and clamped a hand on the opening of her jeans pocket.

The woman backed into a comfortably decorated room with a beige tile floor as littered with toys as the yard had been. She gestured to a pair of wicker chairs in the far corner by a sliding door overlooking a yard that didn't have an adult pool but did sport an inflatable kiddie pool with an enormous blow-up unicorn bobbing on its surface. She plopped into one of the chairs, the toddler still gripping her pocket and the baby sucking on four fingers with big blue eyes trained on me.

I asked for the woman's name and if she minded me recording our discussion. She looked alarmed by the suggestion. "It's just my lamentable memory," I explained.

"Oh. Okay. I guess. What can I help you with? My name's Trina. Trina Wilson," she tacked on in afterthought.

"Thank you, Mrs. Wilson."

"It's . . . just Miss. But please, call me Trina."

"Trina, do you know Pastor Winston Price?"

She wrinkled her nose as if smelling something offensive. "Not personally, but I know of him. I've spoken to him once, but that's it."

"Were you here at home on Sunday afternoon or yesterday?"

"Kyle took us to the beach on Sunday. Kyle's my boyfriend. But I was home all day yesterday. What's this about?"

"Did you see anyone working in the church yard yesterday?"

"Not really. I mean, I did see a couple guys leaving late in the afternoon, but I was kind of busy. With these two." Trina glanced at her children. "One man was tying a ladder on his truck. I figured they must have been doing some maintenance work on the church."

"About what time was that?"

"I don't know. Five. Maybe six. I might not have noticed at all, except the truck was parked on the front lawn instead of in the parking lot."

"Could you describe either man for me?" I asked.

Trina looked out the slider as if the bobbing unicorn might have an answer, then after a long moment, back to me. "Not really. They were both kind of tall. One white. One African American maybe, or a guy with a super dark tan and dreads. The white guy wore a ball cap, so I don't know what color hair he had. Didn't see his face either. The dark guy had black hair, but that's all I remember seeing. I wasn't really paying attention, like I said."

"What color was the hat? Did it have any insignia on it?"

"It was camouflage. You know, like an army uniform. So was his shirt."

Not surprising considering the content of the graffiti.

"Was the other man similarly dressed?"

"No. Shorts. Like the kind surfers wear and a tank top."

"And the truck was parked on the lawn? Anything you remember about that?"

"It was red, but I don't know much about makes of trucks and such. There was another truck in the lot, though. Looked like the sort of van you can rent from Home Depot. With roof racks on top."

Finally. A piece of useful information.

"But you didn't see either man earlier or see them doing any work at the church?"

Trina shook her head. "The kids." She shrugged. "I only saw them when I did because Kyle called to say he'd be late for supper and to make sure there were no toys in the driveway when he got home. So, I went to the window to check. Stevie. He's my oldest boy, he likes to ride his bike out there, and Kyle gets angry when Stevie leaves the bike in the driveway."

I sighed. Two tall men. One Caucasian wearing camouflage. The dark guy in board shorts. Might have been African American. Might have been any guy with a dark tan and black hair. "Have you seen any of the graffiti that someone's been painting on the church?" I asked, changing tactics.

Trina snickered. "I liked the prick. Fit Price perfectly. Yeah. I've seen it all. I can't believe someone had the cajones to paint that soldier thing, though. All over all that glass no less. Had to be the guys I saw, but I didn't notice the painting. Not at the time. I can't believe I didn't notice that artwork then. If you find out who they were, let me know. I'd like to shake their hands. My brother died over there, and Pastor Price was at his funeral. Uninvited."

Her eyes welled with tears, but she stuck her chin out and met my gaze square on. "That A-hole deserves all this and more. So do the jerks who follow him around like trained dogs.

We discussed earlier instances, and while it was clear Trina Wilson applauded every inch of the painted insults, she didn't have any more information for me.

I thanked her and headed for the door with her trailing behind me. She watched from her stoop as I crossed to the next house down but had disappeared by the time I decided no one was home.

Back at Rafe's cruiser, with neither he nor Paul in sight, I leaned against the fender and searched for a number for Home Depot. How many trucks could they have rented out over the last weekend that fit Trina Wilson's description?

With a jolt of dismay, I remembered an orange and white van in Ty Anderson's driveway on Sunday afternoon. And the fact that Ty drove a red pickup truck. Of course, so did a hundred other men in St. Augustine. Including my friend Seth.

CHAPTER 6

RAFE AND PAUL HAD GLEANED NOTHING from their canvass of the neighborhood so we opted to head back to Central where Paul would start the paperwork. Rafe and I detoured to Home Depot to attempt to nab the rental information without a warrant.

I drummed my fingers on the counter waiting for the rental manager to appear while Rafe inspected a pocket gadget every man needs to carry.

"Made in you-know-where," he muttered slipping it back into its slot in the display. "Fall apart the first time you use it, I bet."

A short guy, belly protruding over his belt and hairline receding, approached. "Someone said to go ahead and give you the information you asked for. If you'll step around to this side?" He edged past Rafe and began tapping on a keyboard.

Rafe and I moved to look over his shoulder as he scrolled through a list of vehicles.

I stabbed a finger toward the screen at a panel van equipped with a roof rack. "That's the kind of truck we're looking for."

The man fiddled with the mouse again and a short list popped up, four names long. He started to rattle them off.

I pulled out my phone and snapped a photo of the screen while Rafe's thumbs jabbed away, taking notes on his phone.

"That all you need?" the manager asked.

We thanked him and headed out. While Rafe drove, I enlarged the photo I'd taken and began reading. "Dereck Gilmore. Rented

Saturday, returned Sunday at two pm. Rules him out. Al Perez. Not yet returned. Debbie Duncan. Also, still out. And—" My heart stalled. "Tyson Anderson. Picked up on late Saturday, returned this morning."

No way it could be Ty. He wasn't that kind of guy. A high school counselor with an easy-going personality. Surely, this was just a coincidence.

Back at Central, Rafe went off to check on our fellow detective, Paul, while I began tracking down alibis. Eager to check Ty off the list of persons of interest, I began with him.

He picked up on the first ring. "Ty here."

"Hi, it's Jesse. I'm sorry I didn't get a chance to check in with y'all yesterday. See how you were doing."

"You might not've found anyone here, even if you had stopped over. Natalie was out back at Ryan's place . . ." Ty swallowed back whatever emotion he felt, then went on. ". . . cleaning stuff out to move Dad in. I was running Goodwill and dump errands with stuff dad wasn't bringing with him. Took some of his furniture to Betty Griffin House. Then brought the rest home. We all crashed early."

A tiny sigh of relief. Moving Ty's dad was the reason for the rental. "Well, that's what I'm calling about. I'm following up on a list of trucks rented out at Home Depot. Your name was on the list. Don't take it personally, but is there anyone who can vouch for you between Sunday afternoon and this morning?"

"Off and on, yeah. What's this about?" Concern filled his voice.

Tell him or not? "Someone matching your general description was seen in front of Church of Peace on Monday afternoon. I need to know if you had any reason to visit the church or its pastor."

Ty snorted. "That jerk? Sorry. Shouldn't have said that. But no, I hope never to see that man again. Anywhere, or under any circumstances. Jesse, what is this about?"

"Are you any kind of an artist, Ty?"

"Hell, no. You need to talk to Natalie for that, but you haven't answered my question."

Time to level with my friend and neighbor. "Graffiti, defacing the

Church of Peace. Most recently, the image was of a soldier's helmet, boots, and rifle. A truck like the one you rented was seen on site during the time frame the artist was doing his or her thing. Also, a red pick-up truck."

There was no telling what went through Ty's mind. That I didn't trust him? Or maybe just some deep sense of justice playing out? "Not that I ever would do such a thing. But to answer your question, most of the time I was with my dad. Or rather he was with me. One of his neighbors and their son helped me with lifting the heavy stuff. Bob Nolan. Kid's name was JR. That what you need?"

My shoulders sagged. I hadn't realized just how tense I'd been making this kind of call to a friend. "I didn't really think you were involved, Ty, but I had to rule you out. Tell Natalie I'll see her soon. Give her a hug for me, will you?"

After I hung up, I slumped back into my seat. Damned that was awkward, but one down and three to go. I sprang forward and snatched up the phone.

Maria Perez reported that her husband had rented a truck to move the last of their personal belongings to their new house in Georgia. Al was planning to return the truck to a Home Depot up there while she stayed behind to clean their old house. She'd follow him up later in the family car with the kids. She wasn't sure if the truck had been returned yet or not.

I looked up the number of the Home Depot in Brunswick, Georgia, and a few minutes later I hung up and crossed Perez off the list. Their computers had been down due to a power outage when the truck had been returned around noon on Monday which explained why it still showed as out when I stopped at our local location.

Debbie Duncan didn't answer the number listed. I decided not to leave a message. Trina had described the person she'd seen as tall and a man. So, likely Ms. Duncan was a dead end. Still, I didn't care to leave a message and give her a heads up. Elkton wasn't that far away for me to drive.

Rafe slipped into the room and dropped into his chair. I started to outline the results of my calls, then noticed the pained look in his eyes and the whiteness of his lower lip pressed hard under his front teeth.

"What's wrong?"

He released the death grip on his lip. "My dad had a heart attack. Mom doesn't know if he's going to make it."

Jesus, Mary, and Joseph! Shock hit me like an icy wave. "You need to go, Rafe. Right now. Are you all right to drive? I can take you." The graffiti issue could wait.

Rafe stood. "Gene is going take me." Eugene was one of Rafe's surfing buddies. "I'll leave my notes for you." He pulled his tablet out, tapped at it a bit. A moment later my phone dinged as the information transferred. "Sorry to leave you hanging . . ."

I surged to my feet and hugged him. "Call me if you need anything. Anything. I mean it. And . . . stay in touch."

With an uncharacteristic display of emotion, he knuckled away a tear. "I just hope I get to tell him . . . last time we talked wasn't too friendly."

"Go." I rubbed his shoulder affectionately, then pushed him toward the door. "I'll pray for you, your dad and your mom."

Rafe gave me a rueful half grin. "I'll pray for you, too. Broussard is teaming you up with Zack if anything big goes down while I'm gone."

Before I had a chance to process that bombshell, my cell rang. I answered without looking at the screen.

"Quinn."

"I'm in trouble."

I jerked the phone from my ear and looked at the screen. The frightened voice was my neighbor, Natalie, sounding nothing like herself.

"Where are you? Are you hurt?"

"I'm afraid they're going to arrest me."

CHAPTER 7

MY HEART SHOT INTO OVERDRIVE at the sound of my neighbor's panicked voice. "Where are you?"

Natalie's voice rose to a squeak. "The sheriff's office. In a little room that looks like the kind of place they take criminals to interrogate them."

The day just went from bad to worse. I grabbed my jacket off the back of the chair and rushed out the door, phone still to my ear. "Have they told you why they brought you here?"

"I brought myself. I thought I was doing the right thing. Ty told me he'd take care of it, but I didn't listen and now . . . and now—" She sniffed.

Now I was confused. She turned herself in? "Why exactly did you go to the sheriff's office? Never mind, I'll be there in a few seconds. Hang on."

A quick stop at the sergeant's desk and I was directed to Natalie.

She greeted me with shaking hands. "Rosie's still in the car."

"Calm down and explain." I eased her back into her chair. It was overcast and cool. The dog could wait in the car. "Start at the beginning."

Natalie gulped a steadying breath of air. "I was cleaning Ryan's apartment and getting rid of stuff no one wanted or could use and bagging it up for Ty to take to the dump and I found it. I just didn't know what to do with it. Ty said—"

"What is *it*? What did you find that has you so upset?"

"Some kind of explosives," she squealed.

Holy crap! The hair on the back of my neck rose. What was Ryan doing with explosives? In his little backyard apartment? Less than fifty feet from my house? "What did Ty say about the explosives?"

"He said he'd take care of it. He knows about that kind of stuff from his time in the Navy. But then he got busy arranging furniture and getting his dad settled in and I didn't want it in the house. So, I brought it here. I thought the deputies would know what do to with it."

I relaxed a bit . . . if Ty wasn't worried . . . "Smart move. But I can see why they are a little nervous until they get it sorted out."

"But Rosie's in the car and they won't let me get her out. And that stuff is in the car with her. They're waiting for the bomb squad, but what if Rosie messes with it and makes it blow up?"

I stifled a laugh. Maybe this would all be funny later in the retelling, but right now Natalie was probably envisioning her puppy setting off a nuclear event and it was freaking her out. "Let me see if I can spring Rosie. I'll be right back."

At the sergeant's desk I explained the problem. The sergeant shook her head. "It's your call. Your body parts if it goes boom, but yeah, go get the dog if you think you need to."

"Well, it got this far without blowing up. I'll take my chances." I saluted and left.

The afternoon sun blinded me as I stepped outside, so I shaded my face with one hand, looking for Natalie's vehicle. Then I saw the circle of orange cones with a deputy standing guard. I headed toward him just as the bomb squad rig rolled up.

"There's a dog in the car," I told the first man out of the armored vehicle.

Rosie plunked her paws on the windowsill and panted. No notion of any danger.

With a frown the man strode to the car and peeked in while Rosie tried to lick his face. After a moment, he lifted her out and brought her back to me. "Lucky pooch," he muttered before he turned away, his men already beginning their inspection.

I skedaddled. "Well, girl, an exciting afternoon for you, huh? That'll teach you to beg for a ride next time your momma goes out."

Natalie surged from her chair and snatched the little Boston Terrier from my arms. "Rosie," she muttered, burying her face in the dog's fur.

A moment later the desk sergeant appeared with a bowl of water and a smile before disappearing again. After lapping furiously for several moments, the dog returned to her mistress and settled at Natalie's feet.

"So?" I plopped into a chair next to Natalie. "Suppose you tell me what you know about the stuff you found."

She picked the dog up and cuddled her. "They were in a box in Ryan's closet. If I'd known he had stuff like that out there I'd have tanned his hide." Her eyes welled with tears as the sudden realization that Ryan was gone forever hit her anew.

I patted her shoulder, waiting for her to collect herself.

Natalie pulled a tissue from a box I pushed her way and mopped her face. "I should have listened to Ty. He knows about explosives. I just wanted it gone. Now they're treating me like a criminal."

The room might give that feel, but there were no cuffs and no guard at the door. "They just wanted to get the bomb guys over here to evaluate things before they dispose of the devices. They'll let you go as soon as they're done. And they don't see you as a criminal."

Natalie harrumphed. "They asked me a gazillion questions. It was scary. I didn't know the answers to any of them."

"I'll wait with you, but I have to make a phone call first."

She nodded and I stepped out into the hall to call Paul to give him the information I'd collected and explain where I was.

Forty-five minutes later the bomb techs cleared her car and cut her loose.

I escorted her out and watched her drive off, both relieved and happy to be rid of Ryan's stash. Whatever reason he'd had for keeping it in his quarters he'd taken to the grave. As I turned back toward the building, Paul appeared.

"What's next?" he asked.

"Time to track down Debbie Duncan?" I glanced at my watch. "Your vehicle or mine?"

Ms. Duncan took me by surprise. At least six feet tall with broad shoulders and a butch haircut, she could easily have been mistaken for a man. The African American woman was wearing a pair of men's striped board shorts and a tank top that showed off an impressive set of muscles. The rented Home Depot truck remained in her driveway with half a load of kitchen cabinets still aboard. The other half were stacked randomly around the empty kitchen awaiting installation. The project had taken a back seat to the party she appeared to be hosting.

Debbie Duncan, fresh out of the military and flanked by half a dozen fellow Marines who'd likely come to help with the installation, informed us she'd been here at the house since she'd picked up the truck and cabinets on Saturday morning. She had a solid alibi. Six of them.

We left them still celebrating and headed back into town.

"Maybe it wasn't Home Depot." Paul's brow furrowed. "Maybe your witness saw orange and white and just guessed. U-Haul rents trucks with the same color scheme."

"Well, damn," I said as I pulled back onto Route 207.

Paul's phone rang and he answered it. "Acosta."

He listened a moment, then slapped his hand against his thigh, catching it on the edge of my computer mount and cursed. "Holy shit! Sorry, it's just—" He listened for a bit longer, then clicked off. "The Church of Peace just blew up."

I gaped at him. "No way." I headed for the next turn around. A ladder truck roared past, lights and sirens blaring, followed by a St. Johns County cruiser, and a rescue truck. I flipped on my lights and gunned it to catch up.

Grimly, I drove past scenery we'd already been by several hours earlier, zipping past slower motorists. As we neared the scene, two deputies were directing cars to turn around while a third dropped cones across the entire width of 207. Clearly a tangled mess and no one was going anywhere any time soon. I stopped at the end of a private driveway two doors down and scrambled out.

Flames and smoke roared into the sky, scorching the oak and palm trees surrounding the building. Firefighters swarmed, hooking up hoses and training streams of water on the blaze. Heat from the inferno reached all the way across the street to where Paul and I stood in shocked awe. The scent of burning wood and scorched dry foliage filled the air. My ears were assaulted by shouting men, the crackle of flames and the hiss of water becoming steam.

That magnificent edifice of glass along with its most recent graffiti had completely shattered. What remained of the crystal chandeliers flickered through the waves of flame coming out of the sanctuary.

"Jesus, Mary and Joseph," I muttered as I stared in dismay at the scene. "Pastor Price must have royally pissed someone off this time. Apparently, graffiti wasn't getting the point across."

Two more fire trucks arrived, followed by the fire chief's car.

A familiar face headed our way. "Didn't expect to see you here so soon, detectives." Deputy McKenzie nodded at us. "Do you believe this?"

"Every time I see you, something major is going down, Mac. Does trouble always follow you? Or do you chase it?" I scanned the clusters of gawking spectators. "Where's Pastor Price? Has anyone contacted him yet?"

Mac kept his gaze on the burning church. "He hasn't answered his phone. But there's an elder or whatever he's called here. Robert Angstrum." Mac pointed to a man of about sixty, his white head visible over the knot of people he stood with. Even from this distance, I could see the tears running down his face. A man I'd seen at Ryan's funeral.

"I guess we should go over and let Angstrum know we're here to help. Not that arson will be my case, but—"

"Oh, I wouldn't be too sure about that," Mac said with a grimace. "The firefighters can't get to it at the moment, but there's a body in that hellhole."

CHAPTER 8

THE BLISTERING HEAT HAD SUBSIDED, and the air was filled with the stench of burnt lumber and paint. Wisps of smoke continued to writhe off the carnage, and the cooling embers crackled as the ME's van pulled up in front of the remains of the Church of Peace. Sergeant Broussard and Lieutenant Ward pulled in behind the van, exited Ward's unmarked car, and headed my way. With Zack Oliver.

My partner's warning about working with the arrogant boor rang in my ears. I'd saved his butt two months ago, but that had only humbled him for a couple weeks. Now he was back to business as usual, operating as if women in law enforcement belonged at a desk.

"Lieutenant. Sergeant." I nodded at my superiors. "Zack." I reluctantly offered the greeting.

Our photographer, along with one from the fire department were circling the smoldering embers, snapping from every angle. Sandeep, our ME, followed Mac through the rubble, with bag in hand, to a body crumpled beneath the massive stone altar.

"My case?" I asked the sergeant, refusing to glance toward Zack.

"You and Zack," he confirmed. "With Paul to help out if you can use him."

God help me. I pulled my phone out. "I'm taking a few shots." I strode toward the blackened church. I'd treat this just like any other case, even if I did have to deal with Zack thinking he could do it better.

Zack caught up to me. "You see it happen?"

"I didn't see the initial explosion. Can't prove there even was an explosion. That's just what someone told Paul." I played nice and shared what I knew.

"This morning Rafe and I came with Paul to follow up on a graffiti complaint by the pastor. When we heard about the fire, Paul and I had just interviewed a woman about a truck that might have been involved with the graffiti and were just a couple miles north of here. By the time we got turned around and got down here, the fire was well underway. A neighbor called the fire in."

Zack lifted his aviator sunglasses and squinted at the gaggle of onlookers. "The neighbor see anything helpful?"

"He was out walking his dog when he heard the blast and saw the entire glass front of the church explode. I spoke to him briefly before they took him to the hospital. He needed sewing up from a couple dozen lacerations."

"What happened to the dog?"

My stride faltered. Was there a softer side to this man? "Deputy McKenzie handed the dog over to the guy's wife. Mutt was unhurt, from what I was told."

"Good to know." Zack dropped the glasses back into place.

We reached a pathway through the rubble and picked our way toward the altar. I'd opted for my new fall suit on a day I'd expected to spend at my desk, but the last thing I was about to do was give Zack the satisfaction of a complaint. I glanced down at the soggy black ashes clinging to my favorite loafers and prayed they were not beyond the ability of polish to remedy.

Zack had his phone out, snapping photos as well. "I'd have thought an explosion would've demolished more."

"One of the firefighters said the entire front of the building being glass was likely responsible for that. Shattered easier than brick or stone and released the force of whatever was used to set the explosion." I snapped off a couple photos of the soaring arches that had once supported the roof. Finally, I turned my attention to the stone altar and the body partially shielded beneath it.

Pastor Winston Price. Amazingly intact and still dressed in the expensive suit he'd been wearing that morning. Sooty and far worse for wear, but not burned, or even singed.

Zack brushed past me and squatted next to Sandeep.

The pastor's once handsome face was a sickly gray and streaked with soot. But even more disturbing was the ugly crease marring his high forehead. Something far more deadly than shards of glass had taken him out, probably before smoke could do the job.

Sandeep peered over at my new partner. "Your case?"

"Would I be here if it wasn't?" Zack straightened, tilting his head to inspect the stone altar and the heavy cross now leaning against the end, having fallen from its place suspended from the ceiling.

Sandeep wagged his brows at me and mouthed the words, "Good luck."

A large, ornate book stand turned on its side sat half buried in rubble, presumably for a Bible that was nowhere in sight. I snapped a few shots from various angles, then moved on to the cross. I visually followed the path it must have taken when it fell. Could that have been the cause of Price's bashed skull? Solid oak and over ten feet tall, I would have thought it would decapitate the man. Wouldn't that be odd if his demise was at the hand of the God he professed to worship?

"That what bashed in his skull?" I asked Sandeep, pointing to the cross.

He shook his head. "Wouldn't be any head left if that came down on it."

Maybe it was the Bible stand that did the good pastor in. I panned the wreckage of the once glorious sanctuary. Not a single window left in place. Not much of the roof other than the massive arches. Cushions still smoldered in the sturdy oak pews. The burnt stench made my throat hurt.

"I'm guessing he didn't feel whatever hit him," Sandeep said.

I turned my attention back to the dead man. "Because?"

Sandeep gently turned the man's head to one side, revealing the exit wound of a small caliber round. "Gun shot." The doctor returned the head to its original position and traced the ugly divot on his forehead with his forefinger, stopping at the barely distinguishable entrance of that round. "I'll know more after I get him back to autopsy."

"We'll check in later. Thanks."

With nothing left to be learned, I made my way back to the trampled, soaking grass.

Zack joined me. "Might as well question the gawkers. See if anyone knows anything."

"Sounds like a plan," I agreed. "Where do you want to start?"

The sun was setting before we completed interviewing the watchers. I relayed the lack of information I'd gained from the church elder, Robert Angstrom, before Zack arrived, and we agreed to call it a night.

I took charge before Zack could issue orders. "I'll interview the secretary first thing in the morning. You attend the autopsy?" The hours spent watching Sandeep dismantle the innocent young girl who'd taken her own life still fresh in my mind, I prayed Zack would take this one.

He pressed his lips together, but then nodded. No telling why he chose to agree. Maybe he was trying to play nice, too … ya, right!

My phone rang. Elliot. What the hell did my ex want now?

"I'm kinda busy," I answered.

"We need to talk." Elliot wasn't taking no for an answer.

"I'm just starting a new investigation," I countered. Zack gave me a glance and moved away.

"All the more reason we need to talk. Now" Elliot even firmer.

I sighed as the firefighters rolled up their hoses. "Fine. Your place or mine?" I knew what this was about. A subject I'd been avoiding. Our daughter and her current disenchantment with me and my career, and the boy she'd been caught making out with when I was not there to chaperone.

"How about The Reef? My treat."

Shrewd. He picked a classy restaurant to ensure the discussion stayed civil. But then, they had a salmon dish I loved and rarely had a chance to enjoy any more. "An hour?" I offered. A stop at home to change was a necessity. Everything on me reeked with the scent of smoke.

"An hour," Elliot confirmed. "Please don't keep me waiting."

"That's not fair." I'd danced to his drummer our entire marriage and I'd never kept him waiting. More like the other way around. But he'd hung up and didn't hear my protest.

I waved to the remaining deputies putting up crime scene tape and followed Zack to where we'd left our vehicles. I'd forgotten all about Paul until I found him reading texts on his phone, his butt resting against my fender.

Paul pocketed his phone and climbed into the passenger seat. "What do you want me to do next?"

I put the car in gear. "Go home to your wife."

"And tomorrow?"

"I don't know. Whatever you were going to do before the church blew up. Track down the possibility it might have been a U-haul rental," I answered, my mind still distracted by the coming discussion with Elliot.

Paul subsided into silence while my mind raced to figure out what Elliot was up to. He sounded calm and offhand, but he had something up his sleeve. I was sure of it. And I probably wasn't going to like it.

CHAPTER 9

AS URBANE AS EVER in dark gray slacks and a collarless linen shirt, Elliot stood as the hostess escorted me to a table on the Reef's outside deck overlooking an already dark Atlantic Ocean with a glittery path of moonlight etched against the blackness of the waves. Despite my efforts at home, I felt like a frump. Still in role, Elliot pulled my chair out for me. I sat, already at a disadvantage, whatever this confrontation was about.

"I know what you're going to say," I began as soon as the hostess moved away.

"I doubt it," Elliot responded, "But let's order first."

My appetite would disappear before he was finished flaying me for letting my career distract me from my job of mothering his teenage daughter. But rather than argue, I studied the menu and selected a starter. I made note of a dessert to order later. If there was a later. No point letting Elliot off the hook cheap.

A sharp young man in black slacks and white button-down shirt, sleeves rolled up halfway to his elbows, approached. He flipped and filled our water glasses, noted Elliot's martini, and asked if I would like a drink.

Nope. I needed my wits about me for the upcoming duel.

The waiter took our order and left, probably envisioning us as a lovely couple enjoying each other and the romance of the moonlight on the water.

Time to get this mission started. "Things got a little crazy last month. I wasn't there to see that Jacqui didn't invite that boy to her bedroom, but it won't happen again."

That *boy* had been closer to being a man, and an unsavory one at that. Jacqui, a gullible innocent eager to be twenty-one instead of thirteen, had been grounded for a month.

"Jacqueline has asked if she might live with me."

Words escaped me. Elliot had derailed my pre-planned argument.

Jacqui voiced the same idea with me after I'd banished a male companion from her bedroom, but Elliot had a twenty-something girlfriend. He'd want no part of having a teenager disrupting his love-nest. Just the name, Brandy Lovejoy, set my teeth on edge.

"Yeah, well, she can always hope," I replied. "She'll get over being grounded."

"I was thinking about giving it a try."

If I'd had anything in my mouth, I'd have spewed it all over Elliot's creamy white shirt. I'd come to this meeting expecting another lecture on my duties as a mother. Not to argue for custody. "But what about Miss Lovejoy?"

"Brandy is on board."

I hadn't come up with any arguments for this attack. We shared custody per the divorce agreement, but I'd never expected Elliot to have any desire to exercise his rights.

"Hear me out before you start the debate," Elliot said, setting his martini glass down.

Before I could agree or disagree, the waiter appeared to slide a Caesar salad in front of me and the house Asian tuna for Elliot. "Enjoy," he said as he glanced briefly at Elliot's martini glass before turning away.

My heart raced at the approach of a possible major turning point in my life. One I wasn't ready for and would have avoided if I'd known.

Elliot filled his fork, then set it down uneaten. "I get that your new career is important to you, but let's face the fact that there are times when it keeps you out of the house when Jacqueline needs you to be there the most. Your mother and I cannot keep coming to your rescue every time a case demands your total attention. Jacqueline needs more stability. She needs a parent full time."

He was an investment broker. Regular hours. Hours he had total control over.

Jacqui and I used to be best buddies. We'd shopped together. Wandered the beach. Watched the same movies and laughed ourselves silly. I'd totally enjoyed her becoming something of a friend.

Forcing my voice into a calm that didn't match the tumult in my gut, I countered. "A girl belongs with her mother." That would have been my mother's argument.

"It's not like I'm proposing to move her to California, Jessalyn. You'll still get to spend a significant amount of time with her. You'll be just a few minutes away when you're at work, no more than thirty when you're home."

I dug into my salad while marshalling another objection. I chewed, then swallowed. "It's not the same."

Before I'd made up my mind to follow the career path my mother, then Elliot, had deterred me from after college, I'd been a dutiful stay-at-home mom. Attended all the parent affairs at school, taken Jacqui to dance classes, listened to her struggles to master the violin, volunteered for activities from Brownies to cheerleading. Choosing law enforcement shouldn't disqualify me as mother and guardian.

"No, it's not the same, but consider it," Elliot continued his obviously well-thought-out arguments. "Jacqueline gets along well with Brandy. And before you jump down my throat, Brandy has not tried to displace you. She's her friend, and they enjoy each other's company. It's a big house. Jacqueline will have her own space, and that includes the bedroom she already uses now as well as a second bedroom we can turn into a study, TV room of sorts for her."

"And what will be the rules for this *space* of hers?" My daughter making out, or worse, with boys, unsupervised, in this space of hers, was all too easy to imagine.

Elliot grimaced. "Look, I'm as distressed as you are by the scene you interrupted last month. Maybe more. I'll be the proverbial father with a shotgun, I promise you. No male visitors with closed doors ever, no visitors except a sleep-over girlfriend after eleven pm. And the thing is . . ." he narrowed his eyes a tad. "I'll be home every night. Every weekend. Regular hours. And when I'm not there, Brandy will be."

A sense of loss gripped me deep in my gut. I was losing the battle. To be honest, my relationship with my daughter had already changed in ways that bolstered that sense of loss. Ways I'd not anticipated. Perhaps they'd been inevitable. A girl becoming a woman. In just four years she'd be off to college, an adult in the eyes of the law. On her own without either Elliot or me to keep an eye on her.

I loved my daughter and wanted what was best for her. But would living with her father be the best choice given my unpredictable schedule? Sure, that's what Jacqui wanted right now, but kids are notorious for making poor decisions.

"Can I think about it?"

"Of course." He almost smirked, but perhaps I mistook the look quickly hidden as the waiter returned with our entrees.

Approaching my driveway an hour later, I jerked the car to a halt and leapt out. Dark had totally descended on our little street, yet, with the motor still running, a sporty little red Mazda with the license plate reading "Scotty" barred my way.

The cocky reporter who owned it lounged against the bumper talking to my daughter.

I scrambled to insert myself between the two. "What are you doing here?"

"Following up on a story." He smirked almost as irritatingly as my ex had. "And your girl has been very helpful."

This jerk was not entitled to my daughter or her thoughts. "Get lost." I pointed toward the main road. "Off my property," I said when he didn't move. "Now!"

Still grinning, Scotty Parker closed his notebook and climbed back into his car.

I turned my back on him. "What was he asking you about?"

Jacqui pouted. For a few moments she'd basked in the attention of someone who had been interested in what she knew. "The Andersons," she muttered sullenly as she turned away.

I grabbed her shoulder and spun her around to face me. "What about the Andersons?"

"About the bomb stuff they had hidden away."

My heart thudded. How had Jacqui learned about the explosives? How had Scotty known? And what was he planning to do with the information? What exactly had Jacqui told him?

"That was none of your business. Nor was it anything you should be talking about with a reporter."

Jacqui gave a dismissive shrug of one shoulder but knew better than to turn her back on me again.

"Reporters are not your friend, and you know better than to gossip."

"I wasn't gossiping. I just answered a few questions. It's not like I invited him here." Her voice dripped with scorn.

"Anything you hear second-hand is gossip."

"It isn't gossip that Mr. Anderson was an explosives guy when he was in the Navy. Ryan bragged about it." She stuck her nose in the air, and it was all I could do not to slap it.

I gritted my teeth and pointed at the house, too angry to put my thoughts into words I'd regret.

Holy Hell! Total coincidence, but chances were that weasel of a reporter would connect a few dots and start pointing fingers. Trouble Ty didn't need or deserve dished out by a clueless kid trying to feel important.

I had bizarre nightmares about Jacqui that night. Confused nightmares involving nosy reporters and a boy named Kinte getting it on with Jacqui in her bedroom. I jerked awake, dripping with sweat, a vision of Jacqui's swollen belly heaving as she gave birth filling my head and a reporter eager to plaster her disgrace on the front page of the Record. Heart still pounding, I flopped back on damp sheets.

Rubbing at my face with a fistful of sheet, I glanced at the clock. Six am. I reached for my cell.

"You win," I said when Elliot's sleepy voice came on the line.

"It's not a win or lose deal, Jessalyn." He might have been asleep, but he grasped my capitulation immediately. He'd have made a good lawyer. "We can discuss the details when you're ready. I'll let you do the telling. In your own way and time. It doesn't have to be today, or even this weekend. Just let me know when to expect her."

Less than twenty-four hours ago the discussion had to be asap. *Now he gives me time?*

"What's your schedule like tomorrow?" I asked.

"Two appointments in the morning, but nothing after that. Last night you were totally against this. What changed?"

I wasn't about to share my nightmares with him. That kind of intimacy dissolved along with our marriage. "Tomorrow is a teacher's conference day. No school. Jacqui would have all day to settle in."

"I guess you'll be busy with that new case you caught over the coming weekend?" He asked a question, but it was clearly meant as justification.

"God, I hope not. But…" I sighed with resignation. "Probably, yes."

"I'll clear my day for tomorrow and make sure Jacqueline doesn't make plans for next weekend." He was being gracious, or more likely had an agenda of his own that didn't include our daughter. I hated being so cynical, but Elliot had given me plenty of reasons.

"Thank you for that. And…never mind. I'll tell her this morning. Expect a very excited call before work that'll change your entire lifestyle." My daughter would be packing as soon as the school bus let her off this afternoon, ready to move in hours. At least it would keep her from talking to reporters. Or anyone else, for that matter.

Elliot had no clue what he was getting himself into. He'd never been a hands-on parent. Hadn't helped with school projects or homework. Hadn't gotten roped into being her taxi to everywhere. Hadn't had a teenager around to compete for attention and mess up his love life.

With a heavy heart, I climbed out of bed and headed to the shower.

A lot of hot water, extra make-up and a cup of strong coffee hadn't made me any more ready to tell Jacqui her fate when she drifted into the kitchen an hour later.

"Is that fresh?" Jacqui gestured to my mug, then looked toward the coffee maker. How long had my daughter been drinking coffee? And how had I not noticed before? Chagrin over my failings added shame to my misery.

"Yup. Have a cup."

Jacqui snapped a glance my way, clearly surprised I wasn't challenging her choice of morning beverage.

"I didn't know you liked coffee," I offered in answer to the unspoken question.

"I don't. Not really. But the caffeine wakes me up." She poured herself a mug and joined me at the table. Then proceeded to add three spoonsful of sugar and a healthy dollop of lightener. That much sugar would have wired me for the day, caffeine, or no.

"Your dad and I talked last night. And again this morning."

She tried to look disinterested, but a tense eagerness gave her away.

"We decided, if you still want to live at his place —"

She was on her feet in a flash. "When?"

Something like a gaping hole seemed to open in my chest, the hurt immense. My baby couldn't wait to leave me. Where had I gone so wrong? When had we stopped being friends?

"Your dad can come for you and your stuff tomorrow afternoon. Since there's no school, you'll have the morning to pack."

My daughter snatched up her mug and danced across the kitchen toward the hall without another word. Not even a *thanks, Mom*.

My cell rang, interrupting my pity party. Caller ID unknown.

"Jesse Quinn," I answered, doing my best to keep the pain of rejection out of my voice.

"I know things about that preacher whose church got blown up."

CHAPTER 10

"YOUR NEIGHBOR, THE MAD BOMBER," Zack said dropping a copy of the St. Augustine Record on my desk.

The Church of Peace, flames soaring into the sky with firefighters scrambling to douse the conflagration filled most of the page above the fold, but tucked along the left side was a photo of Ty Anderson. Beneath my neighbor's solemn-faced image was a short paragraph describing the discovery of explosives on his property followed by his background as a Navy SEAL. A quick glance at the by-line and I seethed.

Scotty Parker had gleaned just enough information from my hapless daughter to point a finger at Ty mixing it with just enough facts to make it past his editor.

I speed-read both articles, then slapped my hand down on top of it. "Ty didn't have anything to do with that explosion."

Zack dropped into my missing partner's chair. "You sure?"

"Of course, I'm sure. I've known Ty for years. Long before I moved in next door to the Andersons. And despite his experience in an elite military unit, Ty doesn't have a vindictive bone in his body. But go question him if you feel the need."

The quickest way to get Ty off Zack's list was for them to talk, and Zack would realize Ty wasn't likely.

"He's on my list of people of interest and I plan to speak to him after Sandeep finishes the autopsy," Zack said with a lift of eyebrows.

"Paul said a rental truck was seen at the church on Monday, the day the new graffiti appeared. Tyler Anderson rented a truck. All just coincidence, I suppose?"

"Yes," I replied dismissively. "As were three other rentals from Home Depot. We checked them all out and they all had alibis. Paul is supposed to be looking into U-Haul today."

"What about the explosives Anderson's wife delivered to the bomb guys here two days ago? More coincidence?"

My jaw began to hurt. I unclenched my teeth and took a breath. "Do you really think if Ty had anything to do with the explosion, he'd leave evidence around at his house to be found by his wife or anyone else? He'd have to be an idiot, and I guarantee he's not."

Zack shrugged and I itched to slap him. First Scotty, then Jacqui and now Zack. I was turning into someone I didn't recognize. "I'm headed out to interview a woman who called me this morning to say she had some unsavory information about the pastor she thought we should know. And then I have an appointment with the church secretary." I got to my feet and headed for the door. "I'll meet you back here after lunch. That work for you?" I exited before he could reply. Rafe and I worked well as a team. Zack and I definitely worked better apart.

I'd met Jenny Harker when investigating another case just a few months previous. That had been the murder of my friend Dan Hoffman's wife, and Mrs. Harker had apparently kept my card. When she read the article about Pastor Price's body found in the wreckage of his church, she'd dug the card out to call. Mrs. Harker was one of those ladies who seemed to know everyone and had a mental file cabinet crammed with information about this city and the people who lived in it. Maybe I needed to cultivate her as an official confidential informant.

The Harkers lived in a lovely older home perched atop the dune overlooking the Atlantic Ocean. I hoped she was an early riser and got to enjoy the incredible sunrise each day. I lived close enough to the beach to see sunrises, but most mornings I was busy getting kids off to school or hurrying to get to work. Other mornings I was dead to the world, catching up on overdue sleep. I should have found a house with a westerly exposure, then at least I'd have enjoyed a few sunsets.

Clearly, my informant had been watching for me, and she stepped out onto her porch before I was even out of my car.

"Detective Quinn." She greeted me with an outstretched hand.

I shook it briefly. "It was good of you to call, Mrs. Harker."

"Please. Call me Jenny. I made a fresh pot of coffee," she offered trotting ahead of me toward her kitchen.

Since I was more than ready for another dose of caffeine, I followed with gratitude.

A pair of mugs adorned with images of the St. Augustine lighthouse sat on opposite sides of the narrow kitchen table with a plate of what smelled like fresh baked almond Danish. Yeah, I could do with a fix of sugar, too.

We went through the ritual of fixing our beverages and Jenny slid a Danish onto a plate for me. I took the time to take a bite and compliment the cook with a sigh of pleasure before launching into the reason I was there.

"You said we needed to talk," I prompted.

She set her mug back down. "We do. I don't know the man that reporter was suggesting might be behind the church explosion, but I do know Pastor Price, and he had enemies. Including his own brother."

I whipped out my little notebook. If Rafe had been here, he'd have been asking to tape the conversation, but I didn't want to put Jenny on guard. Jotting notes with a pen was less intimidating.

Jenny glanced at my hand poised over the notebook and seemed to hesitate. "Some of this comes from my niece and I promised her I wouldn't tell. At the time, that is. But I'm sure she still doesn't want anyone to know her part in this so please, this isn't about her. Okay?"

I had no idea where she was going with her report or what her niece had to do with it, but I nodded and put the pen down. "Okay." I took another bite of Danish instead.

"Madison, that's my niece," Jenny started, then hesitated before going on. "Madison is a student at Flagler, now, but four years ago, back when she was in high school, there was an incident with Pastor Price. She confided in me because her mother tells her daddy everything, and her daddy is a deputy. She was afraid her daddy would do something bad if he ever found out."

Jenny stopped for a fortifying gulp of coffee which, considering it was black, must have scorched its way down her throat. Then she sighed and set the mug down again.

"Madison was a member of AICE. It's a program at the high school for smart and gifted kids. One of the requirements is a commitment to community service. Madison and several of her friends prepared and served meals for the homeless at St Francis House."

I'd heard about AICE because Ty and Natalie's daughter Keisha had been a member, but I didn't know much of the details. Hadn't realized it involved community service. "How does this—"

"Winston Price was in charge of the St Francis group," she blurted. "And he did indecent things with those girls." Her face pinched in disapproval.

"Explain indecent." I grabbed my pen. Could the good pastor be guilty of rape?

"He seduced them," she said, lowering her voice. "Not all at once, of course. But he lured them in with sweet talk and promises. Every girl he wooed thought she would one day be his bride, but then he moved on to the next girl. A lot of broken hearts and lost virginity. He got a couple of the girls pregnant."

I kept a carefully neutral tone. "Girls don't usually kill a man because he takes her virginity or breaks her heart. Or even because they discover they're pregnant," I said. Not that one wouldn't. Or that a girl's father wouldn't do it to avenge his daughter's honor.

"But fathers do." Jenny echoed my thought. "That's what Madison thought her father would do if he ever found out Price had even approached her. Or any of the other girls, actually. It's why she made me promise not to tell Ben or my sister."

"Ben Devers?"

"My brother-in-law," Jenny agreed, nodding.

I knew deputy Devers. He was just the sort of guy who would go after any man who had propositioned his daughter. But that was four years ago. Unlikely he'd have waited this long. Unless he hadn't known until recently. But even that seemed unlikely. Jenny Harker would not have called me to point the figure at her sister's husband.

"I don't know any of the other girls, but Madison does. Maybe someone decided Pastor Price needed to be stopped." Jenny looked at me hopefully.

Steadying my voice against the sudden pulsing of my heart, I said, "It's worth checking into." Molesting young girls was a far more likely motive for killing a man than picketing funerals.

"Just don't say anything to Ben. Okay? I don't want to get him involved."

"What about Madison?" Energized, I needed to know more. A lot more. "Will she talk to me, do you think?"

Jenny fidgeted with her empty mug. Perhaps wishing she hadn't mentioned her niece's name at all. Not knowing if law enforcement asking uncomfortable questions would stir up old troubles. Or new ones. Finally, she nodded. "I guess that would be all right. But if it's okay with you, I think it might be better if she called you instead of you contacting her. I'll give you her number but let me talk to her first. Okay?" She opened her phone and tapped away for a minute, then read the number off.

I jotted it down but doubted with the energy pumping through me that I'd forget it. I had to catch Keisha, as well, to see if she knew anything about Price or any of the girls he'd seduced.

Jenny surged to her feet. "And another thing," She crossed the room, snatched a folded paper off a chair by the door and returned. She flipped through the pages, refolded the paper and set it in front of me.

The obituary page with the photo of a pretty girl circled in red ink. Jenny stabbed her finger at the picture. "She was a member of AICE." The image was of the girl I'd last seen pale and still against the inky black sheets of her bed. A girl who'd taken her own life because her boyfriend had dumped her, if her sister was to be believed.

CHAPTER 11

MY PHONE RANG AS I RETURNED to my vehicle. My head still reeled after listening to Jenny's theory.

My son's grin on my phone screen brought a smile to my face, a respite from the disturbing revelations of sexual misconduct. "Hey, Mikey Mike. What's up?"

"I'm going home with Seth if it's okay," he said. "His twins are going to be down, too. Since we haven't got school tomorrow, we're all going to go work on a Habitat house."

Of course, it was okay. Seth was one of the good influences in my son's life and a little physical labor working on a Homes for Habitat project would be a great way for Mike to spend his day out of classes.

"Do you need anything? Like a change of clothes? I'm stopping at home before I head back to work."

"A pair of jeans and an old T-shirt would be nice. Do we have an extra hammer?"

"I'm sure there's more than one extra hammer in your grandfather's old tool trunk. I'll drop it all by. What are you doing with the rest of today?" Seth would make sure the homework was completed. Thanks to Seth, Mike had caught up to his class the year he struggled with my divorce and his father's abandonment.

"More construction." Mike laughed. "Seth started a tree house for the twins, so we'll be working on that. Hey, Mom, I gotta go. See you later. Love you." He was gone before I had a chance to respond.

As I turned the corner onto my street, a familiar figure, a whole head and a half taller, chatted animatedly with Ty Anderson's stooped father on the lawn between my house and theirs. What the hell was Zack Oliver doing here when Ty would still be at school? Ty was the man Zack said he needed to interview, not Ty's forgetful father.

I jerked my unmarked to a halt and hustled across the lawn to the two men. "What are you doing here?" I pointed an angry finger at Zack's chest.

Zack glared at me. "My job."

I turned away. "Hello, Mr. Anderson. I'm not sure you remember me, but we're neighbors now." I patted the older man's shoulder as his brow wrinkled in distress. "My name is Jesse."

His brow cleared. "Are you a friend of Zack's?"

Hardly a friend, but no need to distress Ty's dad who struggled with the early stages of Alzheimer's. "I work with Zack."

"You're a lady cop" Mr. Anderson's frown reappeared.

"A deputy," I corrected him. We both work for the St. Johns County Sheriff's office.

"Oh?" Now he directed the frown at Zack. "Why were you asking me about Ty? He's a good man and a good son. He was a SEAL, you know." This was said to both of us. "He was an EOD guy. You need to be brave to work with explosives. And smart." Mr. Anderson nodded vigorously.

Zack's eyes widened and he shot me a look full of *told-you-so*.

"Grampa? Lunch is ready." My neighbor's oldest daughter, still down from New York, called out, before she hurried in our direction. "Hi Jesse. And—?" Kiara gazed up at Zack waiting for an introduction.

"Zack Oliver, Miss." Zack stuck his hand out and Kiara grasped it.

"He was just leaving," I said shooting daggers at him.

Zack hesitated, then apparently decided there was nothing to be gained by staying, he saluted, and walked to his car.

I seethed. In his innocent dementia, Ty's dad had just given Zack more ammunition to frame an innocent man for a murder I was sure Ty hadn't committed. I hurriedly excused myself and headed to my house while Kiara urged her grandfather back to the house for lunch.

Fuming, I returned to my own house, got a grip on my anger and rummaged through my father's old tool trunk and found two hammers, one much smaller and likely good for one of the twins to use. Then I climbed the stairs and hurried to gather the clothes Mike had asked for. I stuffed everything into a duffle bag and returned to my car, my lunch totally forgotten.

Ten minutes later, when I knocked on Seth's front door and didn't get an answer, I retraced my steps to the driveway and followed the brickwork path around to the rear where I presumed the tree house was being constructed. Maybe Mike was already at work on that project.

I almost ran into Seth coming down a flight of stairs from the deck above. He carried a tray held up in front of his face with his focus on the steps. I backed up until he got to the bottom and lowered the tray.

A warm smile spread across his face that caused a flutter in my belly. "Hey, Jesse."

"I've got a few things for Mike," I said holding up the duffle bag.

"Leave them anywhere. I'll be right back as soon as I deliver lunch to the crew. I'll fix you a sandwich if you have time. Go on up. It's cooler out on the upstairs deck where there's a breeze."

The tray he'd been holding aloft held a stack of peanut butter sandwiches, a plate of cookies, a bowl of cherries and sweating glasses of lemonade. He gestured with his chin toward the partly completed tree house from which came the uneven tapping of hammers.

I owed Zack a discussion about cornering Ty's dad, so I had to leave. But chances were, Zack wouldn't return to Central straight away either and my stomach decided to remind me the only thing I'd had to eat so far today was a single sugar laden Danish at the Harker household.

The interior of Seth's home was refreshingly neat. It was the first time I'd been inside, but it didn't come as a surprise to find it as tidy as I'd come to know the man himself was. Even the makings of lunch were laid out along the counter in neat rows with military precision. Habit drilled into a person that tended to last a lifetime.

Parking the duffle on a bench by the door, I made my way through the kitchen and family area toward the deck beyond. Furnished with wicker chairs and coffee table, it was as promised: cool with a refreshing breeze. A four-inch loose-leaf notebook lay open on the table, displaying the photo of a boy of about six. I plopped down on one of the chairs and looked closer, wondering if the boy was Seth as a child. The image resembled him, but the caption beneath the photo read Samuel John Cameron, July 2, 1974.

So, not Seth. And not one of the twins either. A brother Seth had never mentioned, maybe?

Seth returned to the kitchen, glanced over his shoulder, and called out to ask if ham and Swiss was okay. I murmured in agreement and turned the page.

A yellowed newspaper clipping clung to the page, anchored by aged adhesive tape. *Boy missing.*

My heart fluttered. I read on, ignoring the fact that I might be poking into something personal.

Samuel John Cameron, age 7, disappeared after a fire in the apartment where the boy lived with his parents and younger brother. Both parents and children were evacuated and transported to Wilmington Hospital for evaluation. Mrs. Cameron was admitted with symptoms of smoke inhalation while Mr. Cameron was treated for minor lacerations and released. The toddler, Seth Cameron, had also been admitted for observation. Samuel was last seen, awaiting a scan for a possible head injury and begging the EMT who had accompanied him into the ER to go back to the apartment to save his puppy. The EMT left the boy with a hospital worker who promised to stay with him until he was taken for the scan, but by the time Lincoln Cameron was released, his son had disappeared. None of the staff had any idea who the EMT had spoken with. The description given was of a white female, approximately thirty years of age, with dark hair and eyes, wearing green scrubs, but all the staff known to be on duty at the time were accounted for and none of them reported speaking with either the boy or the EMT. If anyone has information leading to the boy's whereabouts, or the identity of the woman last seen in his company, please contact Detective Avery Harlan at the Wilmington PD.

I glanced up to find Seth holding a plate out to me. When I took it, he bent to close the notebook and remove it from the table.

"An old story," he said, tossing it onto a chair just inside the door to the family room.

"Was Samuel your bother?" I asked, my ham sandwich halfway to my mouth.

A fleeting shadow crossed Seth's handsome face. "Samuel *is* my brother."

"He was found?" So, what had caused the dilated pupils and wrinkled brow? Perhaps his injuries had been more severe than expected.

With the barest of shakes, Seth didn't meet my inquisitive gaze.

I glanced toward the back of the chair where the thick notebook lay, wondering what filled the rest of those pages.

Seth changed the subject to discuss the house they would be working on the following day.

I barely listened to his description of the new Habitat project on Route 206, my mind still captivated by the notebook and its contents. Apparently, his brother's disappearance had never been solved, yet Seth had never given up hope. Seth couldn't have been more than two at the time his brother disappeared. All these years, holding out hope for a brother he surely couldn't remember.

Was the notebook a collection of photos meant to recreate the relationship Seth had never had a chance to experience? Or was it a compilation of articles like the first; an effort to solve the case law enforcement had never been able to close? This was a facet of Seth I hadn't known before. I itched to dig into Seth's big notebook, but not today. Today I had another mystery to solve. And a temporary partner I had to find a way to work with.

CHAPTER 12

ZACK PLOPPED HIMSELF into my partner's chair which reminded me I needed to call Rafe and find out how his father was doing. His dad hadn't been expected to survive, so it was possible Rafe was busy coping with arrangements for a funeral and the care of his mother who was wheelchair bound, but I needed to call and at least let him know I was thinking of him even if there wasn't much I could do to help.

"Sandeep says cause of death had nothing to do with the explosives or the fire at Church of Peace." Zack steepled his index fingers under his chin, clearly waiting for my reaction. I should be shooting holes in Zack's heavy-handed interview of Ty's father, and I needed to fill him in on Jenny's information.

"So he mentioned at the scene," I said.

"22mm gunshot to the head."

"How long before the fire?" I sat up straighter.

Zack clearly enjoyed imparting that bit of information. "Price was already dead when the fire started. Dead before the explosion destroyed the sanctuary. By several hours, according to Sandeep. And he'd been moved after death. Couldn't have been an easy task." Zack tipped back in the chair and clasped his hands behind his head watching me. Challenging me.

Ty was big enough and fit enough to move a dead body. But so were plenty of other men. Perhaps the father of a disgraced daughter.

Except Zack didn't know that part of the good pastor's history, yet.

"How did you fare with the secretary and your anonymous source?" Zack asked, changing the subject.

"Haven't caught up with the secretary, but I did get a home address, so I'll track her down this afternoon." Secretaries knew everything about what went on in their domains, and I was betting this one knew more than she let on about threats against the good pastor. I pulled out my notebook.

"My source isn't anonymous. Her name is Jenny Harker and she wanted to tell me a few things about our dead pastor that might surprise his congregation. And anyone else who thought him a paragon of virtue."

Zack's chair came down with a thud. "We already knew he and several of his flock had the unpopular habit of picketing the funerals of dead soldiers. Like Ryan Anderson."

I had to get Zack to look at someone other than Ty. "Well, try this on for size. Speaking of unpopular habits, Winston Price apparently enjoyed enticing young women barely past the age of consent into sexual relationships, then dumping them whenever someone else caught his fancy or the girl got pregnant."

Zack whistled. "Jeeze! That puts a nasty spin on things."

Yeah! And gives us a whole new direction to the investigation. "He seduced his own brother's fiancé. The brothers haven't spoken since."

"How long ago was that?"

I consulted my notes. "Six years."

Zack tapped the eraser end of his pencil. "If the brother wanted revenge, don't you think he'd have done something before now?"

I scrawled Wesley's name beneath that of Madison Devers under the heading, *people to interview*. "We can't rule him out."

Zack leaned across the table to peer at my list. "Who's Madison Devers?"

Irritated by his nosiness, I closed the notebook before he spied Kiara's name. "There's a program at the high school for gifted scholars that includes community service. There's a group of kids, all young women according to Mrs. Harker, who prepare and serve meals to the homeless once a week. Pastor Price is the organizer." Making himself look good while casing the options for his next target was my snarky guess. "He goes after young women who are smart but socially awkward. He woos them, beds them, then turns them loose thinking whatever went wrong was their fault. None of them want to admit to their gullibility so it's gone on for years, without anyone catching on. Miss Devers was approached but she saw through the smarmy con."

Zack's eyes widened. "Any relation to Deputy Devers?"

"His daughter."

Zack cursed. "Ben would tear the man apart."

"That was four years ago. Unless Ben only just now found out, I'd doubt he had anything to do with the pastor's recent misfortunes. And we can't tell him about it either." What a shitstorm that would start.

"If she was my kid, I'd want to know." Zack lurched to his feet and paced, his long legs eating up the short distance to the door and back. "I'd rip the guy's equipment off for starters."

"Jenny promised not to tell Ben when Madison confided in her, and I promised not to betray that confidence by telling him now, either."

Zack swung around to glare down at me. "Bad move, Quinn. Shouldn't make promises you might not be able to keep."

I shot to my feet, aggravated by his domineering attitude. He still loomed over me, but I was close enough to prod his chest. We were on the same side on this issue but agreeing with anything Zack said rankled. Besides, all this testosterone shit wasn't going to help us narrow down the possibilities.

"Calm down, Zack. There's nothing to be gained from telling Ben if he doesn't already know, and if we want Madison's cooperation to find out who he might have cozened, we'd better not get her father involved."

"Men who prey on kids should be tossed into prison and the key thrown away," Zack spat.

"Well, this one's dead so you're too late." I'd been seething with frustrated anger ever since my talk with Jenny. But we needed to pull it together and work this through methodically.

Zack took two more angry strides, then flung himself into his chair. "Were any of the girls under sixteen?"

I shook my head. "According to Jenny, he was careful not to go after anyone under seventeen."

Zack peppered me with questions. "How many? That you know of? Any names?"

"No names yet, but one possible." I grabbed the folded newspaper and slapped it into his palm. "This could be totally unconnected, but Mrs. Harker didn't think so. This is the girl who committed suicide. The one Rafe and I followed up on just a couple days before Price was killed."

Zack pounded one fist into the other open palm. "I know you think I'm an arrogant jackass when it comes to women, but we're talking about kids here. The only reason I'm not putting my fist through that wall is 'cause I'd probably break my hand."

For once we agreed on something. Two somethings. He *was* an arrogant jackass, and sexual exploitation of vulnerable kids made me want to break things, too. It was one of the reasons I couldn't watch Law & Order SVU. I saw too much of it in real life to ever consider it entertainment.

Zack did the fist-pounding thing a couple more times. "Turn over a rock and all the bugs crawl out. No telling just how deep this goes."

"At least his reign is over." But now the hard part starts. Questioning young women about their sexual mistakes and digging up their pain and disgrace wasn't going to be pretty.

Zack glanced at the newspaper clipping, then away. Probably thinking the same thought I was. "Where do we start?"

"If she's willing to talk, Madison would likely be more forthcoming with a woman. Mrs. Harker said she'd call Madison and explain and ask her to contact me. In the meantime, why don't you track down Wesley Price while I visit the secretary? We might get a few more leads. We can touch base later?"

"Works for me. I'm supposed to speak with Dallas Hill's wife this afternoon. She's in Virginia at her parents', but she agreed to an interview over the phone." With that he got to his feet and left.

I watched his retreat wondering if he'd really put Ty on a back burner or was just touching all the bases before sliding into home. Then I picked up my phone and tapped Rafe's contact number.

"Hey, Jesse. I've been meaning to call, but things have been a bit crazy."

"Don't apologize, Rafe. How is—" I broke off not wanting to voice the worst-case scenario.

"It's going to be a long road to recovery, but I think Dad's going to be okay. They had to do a quadruple bypass to fix all the blockages. The surgery went well, but he's still in the ICU. I asked for some extra time off. Mom's going to need some stuff done before they let Dad come home. Sorry about leaving you hanging but . . . I know you understand."

"Take all the time you need."

"How did you and Paul make out with the graffiti thing? Figure out who the artist is yet? I bet Zack is frothing having to work a stupid graffiti case."

I settled back into my chair. "You got a few minutes?"

"More than a few. Tell me all."

"There is justice in the world. Sometimes. Paul and I were just interviewing one of the renters of a truck from the Home Depot list when we got news that Pastor Price's church exploded."

"You're shitting me," Rafe said, and I could hear the smile in his voice.

"That's not the best part. Although I guess I shouldn't say this since one isn't supposed to speak ill of the dead, but the pastor is no longer with us either."

"This just keeps getting better." Rafe laughed out loud. "Who finally lost patience with the prick and did him in?"

I filled Rafe in on what we knew to date. I wanted to vent about Zack but decided to keep that to myself.

"You better keep me in the loop, Jesse. But right now, I need to go. The doctor is here to give us an update."

"I'll be praying for your dad and you and your mom, Rafe. Take care."

It was good to know Rafe's dad would be okay and to have a chance to chat with my partner, but I had things I had to get back to, as well.

When I arrived at what remained of the Church of Peace to hopefully interview Price's secretary, or at least, poke around and find some clues we'd missed before, a fire department vehicle sat in the church parking lot. I pulled in next to it and got out, my eyes scanning to see who might also be here looking for clues.

A tall man in jeans and a black T-shirt squatted amidst the rubble inside the crime scene tape. He straightened as I approached, and I recognized one of the fire department's arson experts.

"Hey, Jeff."

He nodded and glanced back at the soggy mess he'd been poking through. "Definitely arson. Accelerant wasn't very effective though, so not an accomplished arsonist. Even the choice of explosives was less than effective if the intent was to destroy the whole building or incinerate evidence of murder." He scratched his head. "Tell your arson squad to give me a call. I'll send them my report.

"If you were looking for her, the church's secretary is over in the office and I'm outta here. I told her not to go anywhere near the church itself or touch anything inside the crime scene tape. I dunno, maybe you won't want her messing with anything in the office either. But I'll leave that up to you." He loped off toward his vehicle.

I headed for the church office. Considering there had been a murder, anything even remotely connected to the church and the pastor should be off limits until our crime scene people were done. But maybe they had already been through the office and cleared it.

I picked my way back in Jeff's footprints and walked around to the side entrance. No tape warning people off, here. Inside the foyer, there was crime scene tape strung across the entrance to the church, but none baring my way to the church office. The sound of someone in the office confirmed the secretary's continued presence.

The woman was not nearly as cheery as she'd been the last time I'd seen her. Her face hung in devastated folds, her eyes ringed with dark circles and filled with pain when she looked up from the files spread out on her desk, some just damp around the edges, some far worse.

She frowned. "I'm sorry. I forgot your name?"

"Jesse Quinn." I showed her my star as I scanned the office. "Anything worth salvaging?"

She sagged back into the desk chair. "Who would do such a thing?"

Was she referring to the destruction of the church or the death of its pastor? "I was hoping you might have some ideas."

The tired eyes widened. "Me? I don't know anyone who would do this." She waved a hand toward the door and the rubble beyond. "Wasn't the graffiti enough? They had to destroy the church?"

"Other than the graffiti, were there verbal threats or perhaps threatening emails?"

She pressed her lips together and glanced away.

"Oh, come, Mrs. Ogilvie. Secretaries know everything. They always know more than their bosses think they know." Instinctively looking for another chair, I decided ruining another suit was not worth the respite of taking a load off my feet.

Helen Ogilvie looked near to tears. "He was such a good and godly man. He will be so missed."

He was hardly godly if even half of what Jenny Harker had told me was true. I glanced beyond her to the pastor's office. A laptop sat square in the middle of the massive desk looking remarkably untouched.

"Perhaps you would let me take the pastor's computer with me. If we could access his email, there might be clues."

She jerked to her feet and stared in the same direction. Perhaps trying to decide if she should let me have the computer or if she should protect it from any prying eyes that might be seeking dirt on her adored pastor. In the end, her faith in Winston Price won out. She stepped into his office, grabbed the nearly new MacBook and thrust it into my hands.

Clearly the crime scene techs had already gone over these offices. Evidence of dusting for prints was everywhere and drawers had been opened and not fully shut. But still, an itch to see for myself won out. "Would you mind if I looked around?"

She tried to straighten her soggy files with no luck while considering this, but once again, her thinking came around to letting me do my thing. "I don't know what you think you'll find in there, but . . ."

I didn't need to be invited twice. I wasn't interested in his wall of photo ops. I'd seen them on my first visit, but his desk was another matter. Other than the computer which I already had under one arm, there was nothing on the desk but the desk phone and a small calendar with what appeared to be missionaries at work on a page two days out of date. Who kept a desk that bare?

The pastor's chair was not upholstered so I wiped it off with tissue I found in my pocket and sat down.

The center drawer held an assortment of pens and church stationery, and I was just about to push it shut when the corner of something pink protruding from beneath a box of church contribution envelopes caught my attention. I pulled it out and grimaced at the round girlish handwriting on the pink envelope. When I flipped open the flap, a shiny sonogram image of an unborn fetus fell onto the desk.

CHAPTER 13

HEART RACING, I PEEKED and poked into every crevice and drawer, but nothing else of any significance appeared. I scoured the rest of the drawers with equal lack of success, then moved to the credenza. By now my hands were black with dust, but I was on a mission and barely noticed.

I glanced again at the sonogram. T. Willis and a date more than two years previous was printed along one side. Maybe this wasn't the hot clue it had first seemed. With one last glance at the office and its contents, I stepped back into the secretary's domain.

I thanked Mrs. Ogilvie and promised that the computer would be returned as soon as possible. I thanked her for allowing me to look around and left her still sitting in her waterlogged chair, contemplating the ruin of her world.

My cell buzzed as I slid into my car and secured the laptop in a cardboard box I kept for just that purpose. I pulled out my phone and saw 'Madison Devers' beneath the number I'd logged there when Jenny had given it to me.

"Detective Quinn," I answered as I turned the key and the car purred to life.

"This is Madison Devers. My aunt said you wanted to ask me a few questions?"

"I would like to speak with you. Is now a good time?"

"Sure, I guess. Ask away."

"I'd prefer to talk in person. I can come to you."

This time she hesitated longer but finally acquiesced and gave me an address.

Jenny's niece met me at the door to her townhouse and led me through a spotlessly clean open living area to a lanai with a view of a small pond fringed with dwarf palmetto palms and hibiscus. I wondered if she afforded this upscale place on her own or if someone else was bankrolling it. Her father's salary certainly wasn't comfortable enough unless he was moonlighting, pulling private security for someone with deep pockets. Her mother was a nurse, so her salary probably wasn't generous either.

Had I seen them side by side, I'd never have guessed Madison was Ben's daughter. The deputy was a giant of a man, handsome featured with sharp gray eyes, and a shaved head but owning a fast-growing stubble that gave away his dark coloring. Madison's sandy blonde hair and sky-blue eyes graced a pretty, but unremarkable face, and she was even shorter than my four feet four inches.

She didn't look anything like her mother either. As I recalled from our latest department holiday affair, Ben's wife was almost as tall as he was with flaming red hair and green eyes who looked nothing like her sister, Jenny Harker. Tasha Devers was the kind of woman who turns heads wherever she went. Madison appeared to be a changeling in the family. One with a super sharp brain.

"Aunt Jenny said you wanted to ask me some questions about Pastor Price," Madison said, gesturing to a painted chair with a beachy patterned cushion.

"Thank you for agreeing to speak with me," I responded, taking the offered seat. "I know that part of your life is probably something you've done everything to forget."

The young woman bit her lip and looked away briefly, but then turned back to me with a resigned sigh. "It was a long time ago."

"Your aunt suggested you weren't the only young woman approached by him. He was a sophisticated man who'd had a lot of practice," I offered, letting her know she was not alone, nor culpable of anything but being young and preyed on by someone who should have known better.

Madison lifted her shoulders and straightened in her chair. "I probably should have reported him to Daddy, but I wasn't in trouble, and I didn't want my father to get in hot water if he did something about it on his own."

Smart girl. Ben would have gotten himself in a world of hurt going after the guy to stop him from preying on innocent girls even if his own little girl hadn't been taken in. "Tell me what you remember."

"He made us feel . . ." Madison rubbed the back of her neck as if the memory made her uneasy. Then she squared her shoulders and lifted her chin. "We weren't all that popular. Nerdy never is, I guess. Most of us had never even been on a date with a boy our own age. Then along comes this guy who's handsome and sophisticated and he's treating us like we were special. Not brainy special, but pretty. You know?" She bit her lip, then hurried on.

"He made us feel desired, but we . . . at least I had never been made to feel that way before. Looking back on it, after I wised up and refused to go out with him, I realized I wasn't the only one he made advances toward. Other girls weren't so lucky. They fell for his lies. They thought he was in love with them, and they figured there would be wedding bells next. Kind of dumb for girls who are supposed to be so smart."

The sonogram tucked into the pages of my notebook came to mind. Clearly another young woman who'd envisioned herself married to Price. Just as clearly, one who'd found out the hard way, that Price wasn't in the market for a wife. Or a child.

"Love doesn't have much to do with smart, Madison. They were deceived by a man who had a charming personality and a habit of seducing young women." I almost said vulnerable young women but caught myself. And the charm, I knew, was just an act, but one he had used many times to get what he wanted, which was to get into their pants. That he had a thing for virgins half his age disgusted me. That he'd apparently blown off a girl he'd gotten pregnant sent a cold frisson down my spine.

Madison gazed out at the little pond for a few minutes, then back at me. "Aunt Jenny said you wanted to know who he might have hurt. I'm not exactly comfortable with sharing. It feels like tattling, but considering he's been murdered, maybe I need to get over myself and tell you what I know. I know you need to catch whoever burned the church and killed a man, but I'd like to thank whoever did it." This last was delivered with a thrust of the chin, as if she was defying me to condemn her for championing a killer. Considering the verbal high five from Rafe and my mirror sympathies, I had nothing to fault this young woman for.

"Did you know a classmate named T. Willis? She would have been younger than you but…" I let the question hang.

Madison frowned. Then shrugged. "I don't. Sorry."

I left a half hour later with a list of names. A very short list of definite victims of Price's seduction, but a few more who knew about the affairs even if they personally hadn't been taken in. I still had to talk to Ty's daughter, Kiara, too. She was still at her parents' house, so I'd have a go at her on my own without mentioning it to Zack.

My cell played "The Devil Went Down to Georgia," – the ring tone I'd set for Zack. It was as if my thoughts had conjured him up.

"Considering the most recent graffiti, it seemed like soldier funerals might be connected," Zack said without identifying himself. "But not Dallas Hill's family, at any rate. Hill's wife wasn't all that torn up about her husband's death and he has no siblings. Parents deceased. Graffiti might have been courtesy of some of his military buddies, but I can't prove that."

"Did you speak to Wesley Price yet?" I asked, wanting to keep my own list close to the vest until after I'd had a chance to talk with Kiara.

"I'm on my way to meet him now. How'd it go with Dever's daughter?"

"Seriously doubt Ben had anything to do with Price's death. Madison was up front with me about what she knew and assured me her father never knew anything. She went out of her way not to tell him. Guess she knows her dad pretty well and figured he might go after the guy even if it wasn't her he was defending. Anyway, she gave me a few other names to check out."

"It's late and I've got somewhere to be after I catch up with Wesley. Why don't we meet first thing tomorrow, compare notes and figure out where to go next. By then that geeky deputy might have cracked the pastor's cell and have a list of calls to consider."

Worked for me. "Sounds good. And maybe Paul will hit paydirt with the graffiti tag."

Zack clicked off as unceremoniously as he'd begun the call.

I detoured back up to Central to leave the laptop with our tech guys. It would be nice to have some juicy emails to follow up on. With Mike at Seth's and Jacqui presumably already happily moved into Elliot's, and only a vague recollection of what might be in my fridge, I turned into the Publix parking lot on my way back home. It didn't take long to scoop up a rotisserie chicken and the makings for a salad, and ten minutes later I pulled into my driveway. I glanced over at the Anderson house but decided Murphy needed a walk first. Then Kiara.

My puppy greeted me at the door practically turning herself inside out wagging her tail. But then she caught the whiff of roasted chicken, and my grocery bag became the focus of her attention. I whisked it out of reach, pulled the paper container out of the bag and shoved it into the microwave for safe keeping.

"Walk before dinner," I told the dog as I grabbed a leash from a hook on the wall, then stopped to unholster my weapon and lock it in the safe by the door.

On second thought, glancing down at my polished loafers and neatly pressed slacks, I decided to change first and take my pooch for a walk on the beach. She could swim a bit and work off the energy she'd been saving up. Murphy glanced back at the closed microwave, then trotted after me down the hall and waited while I changed, her tail thumping rhythmically on the carpeted floor. I slipped into my flip flops by the door, grabbed a ball hat that belonged to Mike and headed out Murphy prancing in circles around me.

When we reached the sand, with no one in sight, I unclipped her leash and the dog headed directly for the water. Always taken by surprise by the brilliant colors of the sky in the east while the sun was setting in the west, I stopped to admire the phenomenon before shucking the flips and following the dog to the water.

It was pleasant wading along in the shallow waves as they ran up the damp sand while Murphy checked out every questionable piece of driftwood, shell, or seaweed with periodic romps into the water followed by rolling in the sand. She'd need hosing down before being allowed back in the house. But for now, I decided to let her enjoy herself.

Despite the beauty of the relaxing surroundings, my thoughts inevitably turned to how to best approach Kiara. Madison didn't know if Kiara had ever been involved with the pastor, or even if she'd been approached, but she'd been one of the regulars at St. Francis House. I didn't want to question her with her parents present. If anything had happened back then, but they never knew about it, then let sleeping dogs lie. If they had known, I wanted Kiara's thoughts without their filter. But how to suggest speaking to her privately without raising any alarms?

Kiara lived and worked in New York now, and had only returned for her brother's funeral so I didn't know how much longer she'd be within reach.

Kicking up little sprays of water and enjoying the feel of the waves on my feet, I didn't hear footsteps approaching behind me and felt a jolt of alarm when a jogger passed only feet away.

"Sorry. Didn't mean to startle . . . Oh My God. Jesse. I should have guessed it was you." Kiara turned abruptly, jogging backward as she spoke. She stopped running when Murphy plowed into her, and both went down in a tangled heap on the sand.

"You are a disgrace," Kiara told the soaking wet puppy as she rolled onto her butt and hugged the water-logged dog. Murphy licked her face, returning the greeting.

I reached down to help Kiara. She took my hand but leapt nimbly back to her feet, barely needing any assistance.

"I was hoping to find you at home tonight," I began as I bent to snap Murphy's leash onto her collar.

"You don't have to leash her for me." Kiara lifted the hem of her T-shirt and mopped her brow.

"Thanks. I usually only let her run when we're the only ones on the beach." I put the leash back into my pocket.

Kiara dug into her own pocket and struggled for a moment before tugging a faded tennis ball free. "Look what I found?" she said as Murphy danced circles at her feet. "Sit."

Murphy sat. Kiara grinned and flung the ball into the ocean. Murphy knew the drill and did her best to stay sat but it was as if her rear end was spring loaded, and she had a hard time keeping it on the ground. Kiara finally took pity on the eager dog. "Fetch."

And Murphy was off, charging into the water and swimming toward the distant fleck of green.

Perhaps God had heard my muttered prayer about having a chance to talk to Kiara alone.

"So why were you hoping to catch me at home?"

I swallowed, rapidly hunting for a diplomatic opening, and finding none. "I met with Madison Devers earlier today," I plunged in. "She said you were part of a group from the AICE that served meals for the homeless at St Francis House."

"I used to hang back in high school with the AICE group." She huffed out what might have been a laugh or a sigh. "Meant to stick with it when I went to college, but then I transferred to Cornell and never came back. Mom misses me and I know she hoped I'd stay close, but…"

"I'm pretty sure she's proud of you in spite of living in New York, and she looks forward to whenever you do come back for a visit. Well, maybe not this visit so much, but you know…
Christmas and that sort of visit," I said thinking how empty my house was going to feel tonight without either of my kids there. "But what I really wanted to ask was what you knew about Winston Price's involvement with the meals served at St. Francis and the girls who were part of that group."

Kiara's pretty smile folded up and a hard frown took over her face. "What are you implying?"

"Not implying anything. Just following up on something Madison said. Did he ever hit on you?"

She made a snicking sound with her tongue, very like the one I tended to make that so disturbed my mother. "I was kind of surprised when he tried. I turned him down. He called me an uppity black bitch and never spoke to me again. It was kind of shocking he'd even tried since I'd heard he was something of a bigot."

I was appalled and relieved at the same time. Disgusted that a man of the cloth would use such a racial slur, but wondered if Kiara's light coloring might have misled the man; and thankful she hadn't let herself be deceived.

"Do you remember any of the young women who weren't as discerning?"

"You want names?" Kiara snicked again, then bent to greet the dripping Murphy who'd just dropped the ball at her feet. She repeated the fetching routine and Murphy dashed back into the ocean again. "That dog has more energy than a room full of kindergarteners."

"She's been shut up all day." I didn't repeat my question, not wanting to push.

"I don't think anyone wants to admit they were taken in." Kiara sighed with a sad shake of her head. "Can't imagine any of them wanting anyone to find out just how stupid they'd been. Why do you need to know now? The man's dead and he can't seduce any more gullible girls."

"I'm trying to figure out who might have killed him."

Kiara gasped. "He was murdered? I thought he died in the fire."

"The fire was apparently set to cover up the deed, but it looks like homicide. And I'm trying to figure out who had motive."

"None of the girls I know would kill the man, no matter how badly he treated them, so, I can't see how knowing who he took in would help."

Murphy returned, but this time Kiara was gazing at nothing in particular, certainly not the waiting dog. Murphy whined and finally Kiara looked down, reached for the ball, and threw it again.

"More likely, it was a man. Maybe someone's father or brother. Or even a jealous boyfriend."

Kiara appeared to consider this. "I guess that's possible, but I'm not sure how anything I know would help. I haven't seen the man in over eight years, except—" She snickered but there was a hard edge to it. "Except at Ryan's funeral."

"I hoped you might know who some of his more recent victims were." This time, I scooped up Murphy's ball and sent it bouncing down the beach, the dog in hot pursuit.

"I'm sorry. I don't. Like I said, I meant to continue with the homeless meals, helping out, maybe being a mentor or whatever to newer girls. But then I went to New York. I have no idea who he was pursuing lately. I can ask around and get back to you. If you think it would help."

"It might," I agreed. "Does the name T. Willis ring any bells with you?"

A definite shake of the head. "Nope. It's been a while," she reminded me.

This time when Murphy returned, she dropped the ball and watched it roll slowly toward the water, then plopped down on the damp sand.

"I think we finally tuckered her out," Kiara said with a grin. Then she glanced at her watch and her eyes jerked toward the dunes. "I've got to get going. I've got a Zoom meeting with three study-buddies in ten minutes. Catch you later."

Then she was gone, her long slender legs eating up the distance until she disappeared from sight.

Murphy watched Kiara go, then glanced up at me, her tail thumping, belly still glued to the damp sand. My mind was puzzling over the name on the sonogram I'd found in Price's desk. T. Willis appeared to have fallen between Madison and Kiara's classes and the current crop of AICE girls. Tomorrow I was going to make time to pursue the lead.

I dropped to my knees and buried my forehead in Murphy's sandy wet fur. "It's just you and me tonight, Murph." My heart weighed heavily contemplating a house with no kids. Mike would be back, but not Jacqui. Perhaps not ever to live under my roof again. What had I done, letting my little girl go without fighting for something different?

CHAPTER 14

STANDING IN THE MIDDLE of my living room, the house silent and dead around me, heaviness filled my heart. Signing off on my daughter moving in with her father had been a difficult decision, but the reality was starkly worse. As I sank down onto the couch, a flood of memories washed over me.

A tiny pink bundle just home from the hospital. A fretful baby, emerging teeth aching as I paced the floor in the middle of the night. Wearing braids, a brand-new school uniform and a huge smile on her first day of school. Marathons of cribbage and bowls of popcorn in front of late-night movies. Laying on the beach giggling in the dark before my precious girl reached that threshold of puberty. Where had all that gone?

I'd envisioned this night differently. The house to myself, a warm bath, maybe. A glass of wine, time to unwind without having kids to worry over. The reality was crushing.

There was an open bottle of Reisling in the fridge but getting up to pour a glass seemed like too much energy. And somewhere along the line that leisurely bath had lost its appeal.

Fragments of information gleaned from today's interviews begging to be put into some kind of perspective in my professional life, battled with the overwhelming sense of loss in my private world. I couldn't think beyond the emptiness in my soul.

Murphy padded over and licked what she could reach of my face as if she sensed how lost I felt. I gathered her up into my lap and hugged her warm body close. She continued licking, first my chin, then one ear. That tickled me and I laughed.

"Thanks, Murph. I needed that."

Maybe sitting in the dark was part of the problem. I leaned over the wriggling ball of fur in my lap and flicked on the table lamp. The dog jumped nimbly back to the floor just as my phone rang.

Mike's ring tone. Was he calling to check up on me?

"Hey, Mike?"

"Mom. Where are you? Seth's been attacked, the kids are bawling, the ambulance isn't here yet and—"

On my feet, already headed for the door, heart racing. "Slow down, Mike. One thing at a time. What happened?" I scooped up my car keys and shut the door on my confused puppy. I took the stairs two at a time. "Is he breathing? Can you get a pulse?"

"Both," Mike answered, sounding like he was trying to stay cool but close to losing it. "He's trying to talk. I think. But he won't open his eyes."

Okay, Seth was alive, but what the hell had happened? I tried to gather some semblance of professionalism around me, but my heart refused to cooperate as it galloped and a kaleidoscope of every assault scene I'd been called to paraded across my mind. I swallowed hard and forced a calm I didn't feel.

"Are you and the twins okay?"

"Yeah. We were still inside the house when it happened."

"Seth's house?"

"No. We're at the Habitat project."

The whimpering of two frightened boys was abruptly drowned out by the wail of an ambulance. Thank God! "What's the address"

"I don't know if it's got an address yet. It's on 206 just past the railroad tracks."

Jaysus! A dark and lonely place, but if the ambulance was already there, I'd have no problem finding it.

"What happened." I dropped my cell into its cradle, leaving the line open and spit up gravel as I screamed out onto A1A, cutting off a pickup truck. The driver flipped me the bird.

"Mike? You still there?"

"Yeah." He sounded relieved. Thankful that professionals had arrived, and he was no longer in charge, no doubt.

"What happened," I asked again.

"I don't know. Everyone else was gone and we were picking up our stuff. Seth took his toolbox out to the car but when PJ and I caught up—"

"When you caught up," I prompted. "What?"

"A car was turning onto the road and Seth was just lying there. Not moving. When he wouldn't answer me, I called 911. Then I called you. Then we tried to get him to talk to us. Maybe I should take PJ and Sammy inside the house we were working on? I don't think they should see their dad like this."

No way did I want my son going back into a house with no lights if there was even a slim chance whoever had done this to Seth was still around. "Stay with the ambulance. Maybe move far enough away so they can't see as much but stay with the rescue guys. I'm almost there."

I flipped on my lights and bolted through the traffic light on Route 1. A moment later the flashing of red and white lights appeared, another couple of moments and I lurched to a stop beside the ambulance.

Mike, with his arms around Seth's boys, was trying to get them to move away from the huddle of emergency personnel kneeling around a figure sprawled beside Seth's truck.

I wanted to dash to Seth's side but forced myself to go to Mike.

"He's going to be okay, guys. C'mon." Mike urged the younger boys.

I put my arms around all three. "Mike's right." I prayed God he was or would be soon. "The experts are here to take care of your dad. But you don't want to get in the way. Right?"

One of the twins, I couldn't tell them apart, looked up at me, tears streaming down his face. "But—"

I watched Mike suck in a steadying breath and put a smile on his face. My son, suddenly so grown up. Doing his best to reassure the twins. Saying the same things cops did as they held mangled, and frightened bodies trying to reassure the injured they were going to be fine.

I caught Mike's eye and nodded. He was doing okay. Now I had to hold myself together and do the same. "Let's go sit in my car."

I tousled the twins' hair as I urged them in that direction. "What's your mom's phone number?"

They rattled it off in unison.

"Climb in back with Mike. I'll call your mom." I mouthed *love you* to Mike and turned away.

A county SUV pulled in, blue lights flashing, and my friend Mac emerged.

"We have to stop meeting this way," the young deputy tried for humor before he glanced down and saw who the injured man was. "Oh God! Sorry, Detective Quinn. I didn't know. What happened? Were you here?"

I shook my head. "I probably know less than you. My son was here but he didn't see what happened either. He and Seth's boys are in my car."

I'd promised to call their mother, but I wanted more info first. I dropped to my knees in a sliver of space next to the EMT assessing Seth's vitals.

"Seth? Seth? Can you hear me?"

The man I'd so recently allowed myself to start caring for didn't respond. I groped for his hand and clutched it. "Seth." I swallowed my panic and tried to take a professional appraisal.

No blood, nothing visible in the way of injury. The vitals being rattled off by the medic at my side should have been reassuring, but Seth's non-response wasn't.

"Seth," I pleaded, squeezing his hand. A hand that just days before had cupped my face as Seth bent to kiss me goodnight after our first date. "Seth. Please. Open your eyes. It's Jesse."

"We need to move him, ma'am." The EMT pushed himself to his feet and put a hand under my elbow.

I let myself be urged to a stand but didn't let go of Seth's hand. Three men lifted Seth and slid the gurney under him, jacked it to full height and began rolling it toward the ambulance.

"Seth," I pleaded, hurrying along at his side.

Just as they started to fold the legs and push the gurney into the vehicle, Seth's eyes opened. He looked at me, a frown puckered between his dark brows.

"You're going to be okay," I insisted. Then, with Mac and the entire EMT squad as witness, I bent and kissed Seth on the mouth.

"You have to be okay," I whispered into his ear as the gurney slipped into the back of the waiting rescue truck.

CHAPTER 15

MAC STOOD NEARBY, but far enough to give me some privacy as I punched in the phone number for Seth's ex. When I didn't get an answer, I hung up and tried again in case I'd gotten the number wrong. After four rings, I heard a breathless, "Hello?"

"Is this Annette Cameron?"

"I think you mean Annette Gault." Guess Seth's ex had gone back to her maiden name.

"Is Annette there?"

"Who is this?" A male voice came on the line.

"Detective Jesse Quinn. I'm looking for PJ and Sammy's mom." I was probably speaking to the boys' grandparents, and I didn't blame them for being suspicious of someone who didn't know their daughter's change of name.

"She's not here. Are PJ and Sammy okay?" Urgency in the voice now.

"They're fine," I responded quickly. "But I promised them I'd call their mother. Seth has been injured and—"

"Where are you? Leslie, grab my wallet and keys." This was apparently directed towards his wife who, I assumed, was the first woman I'd spoken with. "How badly is Seth hurt? Where are the boys?"

"Mr?"

"Gault. Philip Gault. I'm Sammy and PJs grandfather. My daughter is out so we came over to feed the animals." Philip Gault sighed.

"Sorry, didn't mean to run on. I guess you need for us to come pick up the boys? But I need to know where you are."

I gave him an approximate location and told him to look for flashing blue lights.

Everything in me wanted to head directly to the hospital without delay, but there would be questions to ask and answer. Mac had a report to submit, and he'd need the time to speak with PJ and Sammy before their grandparents took them home. Then he'd need to question my son.

By the time I'd finished my call, Mac had dropped a bunch of orange cones around the place where Seth had been found and adjusted his search light to better illuminate the area. The driver's door to Seth's red Ford pick-up hung open, but nothing seemed amiss. Other than Seth, who must have surprised someone bent on stealing his truck.

The driveway was as bleak and lonely as I'd envisioned. Just the sort of place that invites that kind of trouble. I swallowed and turned back to Mac.

Together we approached my car where the boys sat, legs dangling out the open door, worried expressions clouding their faces.

Mike clambered out and I stood back while Mac asked Mike to run through what he knew. Nothing I hadn't already heard.

"Can you remember anything about the car you saw leaving?" Maybe the license plate? Or color? Mac asked with calm patience.

Mike shrugged. "It was dark. I wasn't really paying attention. But it was a sedan. Black or maybe dark blue or green. I'm sorry. I just didn't look that close. I was looking for Seth. Oh!" He perked up. "It had a Gators plate. I didn't see the number though. Whoever was driving that car had to be the guy who knocked Seth unconscious. Why else would he just take off when I showed up?"

"And that's all you remember?" Mac prodded.

I had no idea how many cars sported a University of Florida plate. It wasn't much to go on and the likelihood of catching the guy if Seth couldn't remember anything was slim to none.

Mac tucked his notebook back into his pocket. "Every little bit helps, and you did good. Called 911 first, then took care of things. Your mom should be proud."

Before either of us could answer a silver minivan turned in and pulled to an abrupt halt beside Mac's SUV. A man of about sixty climbed out and a woman hurriedly joined him. "Where are my boys?" she asked in a high-pitched voice.

PJ and Sammy were already tumbling from my car and dashing toward their grandparents. The woman hugged them to her ample bosom, murmuring comforting nonsense.

I glanced at Mac. "Do you need to question the kids?"

"They saw less than I did," Mike interjected. They were both inside the house sweeping the floor while I carried out some of Seth's gear."

Mac shook his head. "If I need to speak to them, I'll do it later."

I turned to Mr. Gault. "I know they'll be worried about their dad, but I'll keep you updated. Right now, they should go home with you. Thank you for coming so quickly."

I handed him my card. "According to Mike, they didn't see what happened, but if they remember anything suspicious or anything at all that you think I should know, call me."

"We have a key to Seth's place," Mr. Gault said as he watched his wife bundling the twins into their minivan. "We'll stop and collect their gear on the way home."

I nodded and he turned to climb into the driver's seat. A moment later the engine came to life, and he carefully turned his vehicle around and pulled back out onto 206.

I turned to Mike. "Maybe you should have gone with them and collected your stuff, too."

Mike pulled his hand from his pocket and held up a shiny key. "I've got my own."

I was surprised, but then not surprised. Mike and Seth had become close over the months, first with Seth doing the tutoring and helping Mike get his grades back up, then just as friends as the two worked together rehabbing the old Camaro in our garage for Mike to use once he had his license. Seth had filled so many of the holes in Mike's life that should have been filled by Elliott. Except that the animosity between Mike and his father and Elliot's disinterest had put that father-son relationship in jeopardy.

"In that case, you'll have to wait for me, then."

Another pair of deputies had arrived during this exchange and all three scoured the surrounding area with flashlights. We watched the search but apparently, they found nothing. Whatever Seth had been hit with had been taken with the attacker. The truck appeared untouched.

"The keys are in the ignition," a female deputy said gesturing toward Seth's truck. "I'll take it down to Central to be dusted for prints and get a thorough going over in better lighting. Someone can pick it up tomorrow."

"I can drive it," Mike stepped forward. Seth let me a couple times. I know he'd say it was all right."

"I'm sure he would," I agreed putting an arm around my son's waist. When had the kid gotten so tall I couldn't drape my arm around his shoulders? "But we'll discuss that tomorrow, too."

Mike frowned. I thanked the deputy and turned Mike toward my car.

Once on our way, I began to outline my plan to wait while Mike collected his schoolbooks. Then I'd drop him off and head to the hospital. It had been more than an hour and I was anxious to find out how Seth was.

"I'm going with you, Mom." Mike announced with finality and glared through the windshield, apparently daring me to disagree.

I didn't.

The Flagler emergency room was strangely quiet. I was used to chatter and noise, the hustle of efficient medical personnel and anxious patients and family. Even the television mounted on the wall was muted as Steve Harvey made faces and gestured toward the answer board on a re-run of Family Feud.

I strode to the desk and asked after Seth Cameron.

"Are you family?"

"Yeah. I'm his son," Mike said stepping up beside me. "This is my mother."

The woman's eyebrows rose, but she nodded. "They just took him up for X-rays. They'll probably admit him for observation over night, but he was conscious and aware of what was going on when they came for him. If you wait over there, I'll let you know when and where you can see him." She pointed to a row of vinyl clad chairs.

"His son?" I queried as Mike and I claimed our seats.

"If I'd said I was just his friend, they wouldn't have told us anything."

"They'd have told me. I have a badge."

Mike shrugged. "Well, it worked, didn't it?"

"When did you get so tall?" I looked up, realizing he was taller than I was even sitting down, and he was a gangly kid, all legs. Half an hour ago, I hadn't been able to put my arm around his shoulders. Now he was looking down at me. It seemed as if he'd grown three inches while I slept the night before.

He stuck one leg out for me to see. "Right after you bought me new jeans."

We both contemplated the hem of those jeans well above his anklebone as silence fell between us.

Six months earlier, I'd never met Seth and Mike had only seen him in the halls at school, yet here we were, fretting and anxious as if Seth really was Mike's dad.

Mike's hand dropped over mine on the armrest between us. "He's going to be okay." Was Mike trying to reassure me, or himself?

I flipped my hand over and gripped his. "Let's pray."

No words were spoken aloud as we both sent our requests off to ears that never stopped listening. After a few minutes, Mike disengaged his hand and got to his feet. "You got any change? I'm thirsty."

I dumped all the change I had into his outstretched palm. "I'll take coffee."

While Mike was gone, the nurse appeared. "Your . . ." She hesitated, probably wondering if my introduction as Mike's mom equated to being Seth's wife or not. "Nothing is broken. He suffered a concussion, and is resting comfortably, but is now sleeping and we're keeping him for observation. He asked after his boys?" She looked at

Mike's empty chair. "Room 412."

"Mike's getting a soft drink. Thanks for coming to let us know." No need to set her straight.

Something fluttered against my head, and I jerked awake.

"What am I doing here?" Seth asked, pushing my hair out of my eyes.

I jerked to sit up and blink the sleep out of my eyes. Seth looked remarkably alert. How long had he been awake while I slept with my head resting against his hip? Pray God I hadn't been snoring. Or drooling.

Seth smiled, then frowned as he touched the side of his face. "What happened?"

"What do you remember?" I didn't want to nudge his memory in any specific direction.

The fingers that a moment before had been tentatively touching his temple plunged through his hair and his brows pinched together. "We were working at the Habitat house. I think we were done for the day, but . . . did I fall off something? Where are PJ and Sammy? Are they okay? And what about Mike?" He pushed himself to a sitting position, trying to free his legs from the sheets tangled around them.

"They're fine." I shot to my feet and eased him back onto his pillows. "PJ and Sammy are with their grandparents. I'm sure they'll be down to see you later today. Mike's over there." I pointed to my sleeping son who was draped across a visitor's chair in a way that would have left me limping for days.

"But what happened? How did I fall?" Seth frowned again. "What did I fall off of?"

Whoever would oversee this investigation, it wouldn't be me, but Seth would know soon enough when the detective assigned to the case showed up to question him.

"You didn't fall off anything. You took your tools out to your truck and for reasons we don't yet know, you were struck by an unknown assailant. Mike found you sprawled beside your truck and called 911. He didn't see what happened. Nor did the twins."

Seth slumped back into his pillows. "I don't even remember hauling my tools out to the truck."

"It will come back to you. Maybe not right away." I prayed it would come back. And I prayed he'd seen the guy or at least enough to lead us to identify the assailant.

"You stayed all night?

"In case anyone suggests it, Mike claimed to be your son down in the ER, so they'd let us stay."

Seth closed his eyes, maybe hoping to jog something to the forefront of his mind. I looked at my watch and realized I had a job to get to. Mike needed to get ready for school, and I had a meeting with Zack. We both needed a shower, a change of clothes and something in our stomachs.

My bones creaked from a night sleeping half sitting and half curled against Seth's side. "I'm getting old," I muttered as I stretched.

"In that case, old is beautiful," Seth replied reaching for my hand as I started to move away. "How bad was I hurt?" He wiggled his feet, then his head and winced.

"You've got a hard head. And a concussion. They kept you for observation. At least that's what they told me."

He began prodding his scalp again and let out a soft yelp. "Will you be back if they don't let me out of here today?" His chocolate brown eyes seemed to be pleading with me for more than just my company, but I couldn't fathom what. I dug in my pocket for his cell phone which I'd found after they'd taken him away in the ambulance, then set it on the rolling bed table. I hoped it had enough juice to last until I could bring him a charger.

"Promise," I replied kissing my fingertips then pressing them to his mouth. "Call me after the doctor comes in to see you."

All the things that had gone wrong in my life lately still haunted me, but this man wasn't one of them. When Natalie suggested we were an item, I'd insisted we were not. I'd thought I didn't need the complications of a romantic relationship in my life, but if last night had taught me anything, it was that while Seth might be a complication, I wanted him to stay around.

I roused Mike who jerked awake like a marionette in the hands of a toddler. "What?"

"Time for school. And work."

"Is Seth gonna be okay?" Mike whispered dipping his head in Seth's direction.

I nodded. "Maybe he'll let you use his truck to come over for a visit after school. If he's still stuck here by then."

Mike stopped to speak with his friend and mentor while I went out to leave my card at the nurse's station along with instructions to call me when Seth was discharged or if anything else came up. A moment later Mike loped to my side.

"You're going to catch the guy who did this. Right, Mom?"

CHAPTER 16

ZACK OLIVER HAD TY ANDERSON backed up against his truck, clearly firing questions at him while a deputy I didn't recognize appeared to be searching the bed of the pickup. Natalie watched, her fingers pressed against her lips, panic in her eyes.

I scrambled from my vehicle and stormed across the lawn to confront Zack. "What the hell is going on here?"

Zack didn't even glance my way. "Looking for a murder weapon."

"I don't own any weapons," Ty said with a calm I was not feeling.

"That hasn't stopped other people bent on murder," Zack sneered.

"What are you talking about?" I demanded. "Whose murder?"

"The good pastor. What other murder do we have on our agenda right now?"

I wanted to scratch Zack's eyes out. Picketing a dead soldier's funeral didn't cut it for me as motive. And the circumstantial connection between Ty and explosives was just coincidence.

"Don't say another thing before you consult a lawyer," I told Ty.

"But I didn't do anything. Why would I need a lawyer?" Ty started to move away from the truck and Zack pushed him right back.

"We're not done yet."

"Uh. Detective?" The young deputy I barely knew put his hand on the edge of the truck bed and launched himself back onto the ground. "There's no gun. Anywhere."

"Fuck!" Zack muttered then climbed up into the bed of the truck himself. He burrowed through the tools the younger man had been so careful with, tossing them to the side in a heap as he went.

Ty's jaw tightened. He was a little OCD about his tools, I knew. But he knew better than to give this angry detective any reason to get more upset. Despite the current political climate with so much attention on the mistreatment of black men at the hands of law enforcement, Ty kept his mouth shut.

When Zack finished tossing the contents of Ty's toolbox, he searched under the box, then leapt back to the ground and yanked the passenger door open. He spent the next twenty minutes searching every inch of the interior, pulling the seats up, and pawing through the glove box. Again, coming up empty he slammed the door.

Zack pointed at Ty. "Don't decide to take any trips out of town. I'll be back," he uttered through gritted teeth, then stormed off toward his ride.

"I'm really sorry about the mess," The young deputy apologized.

"Not your fault, "Ty said with a nod.

The younger man hurried after Zack and barely managed to drop into his seat before Zack put the car in gear and took off spitting gravel in his wake.

"What exactly was he looking for?" I asked.

"He said he got a tip that he'd find a gun in my truck."

"Who gave him the bogus tip?" And why hadn't I been given a heads-up?

Ty flexed his jaw. "He didn't say."

I apologized again, echoing the young deputy.

"Not your fault, Jesse." Ty glanced at the space where Zack's vehicle had been parked. "I'm just glad it's you and not me who has to work with the man. Are you serious about getting a lawyer?"

"I believe you, Ty, but Detective Oliver is in a hurry to pin this on someone and close the case. Don't let it be you. I'll find out what Zack Oliver thinks he has on you, but it can't hurt to have a lawyer available and up to speed." I prayed it would be nothing more than merely circumstantial evidence. That along with Zack's desire to close cases as fast as possible and gain momentum for his climb up the ladder in the department. More troubling was who'd want to point the finger in Ty's direction by calling in such a tip in the first place.

"You made any enemies recently?" I asked Ty, who now had an arm around Natalie's shoulders.

Natalie straightened. "Ty doesn't make enemies.

"No one you've had any arguments with lately?"

Ty shook his head.

"I'll get to the bottom of this, trust me. But it sure looks like someone wanted to get to you for some reason."

Ty scratched his still stubbled chin. Apparently, Zack had gotten him out of bed. "Some of the kids I see aren't happy people, but I'm not their problem. I'm just the person they dump some of their frustration on. I don't see any of them pulling a prank like this. And before you ask, I'm not giving you any names. It's a matter of privacy and I'm not going to betray any kid who found the courage to come to me instead of wreaking mayhem somewhere else."

I was aware of the duty to warn guidelines. But in this case, the only one likely to be harmed by keeping quiet was Ty himself. A moral conundrum.

"But you can find out who called. Right?" Natalie interrupted with a militant glint in her eyes.

"I can try." Jesus, Mary, and Joseph! I felt like I had the reins of half a dozen horses all pulling in different directions. A graffiti artist with a hard-on for an unpleasant church pastor. A murder with no leads beyond the graffiti guy we hadn't yet caught up with. Seth accosted for no obvious reason. Ty being fingered by someone who might or might not hold a grudge. I had a blossoming headache and my day had just barely begun. I needed coffee. Badly.

"If you have a lawyer or know one, give him a call and explain what happened this morning. Tell him about Natalie's visit to the sheriff's office, too. Just as a heads-up. In case you need one, it'll be good to have someone who's up to speed as quickly as possible."

Ty nodded his acceptance of my advice. "It's a woman, actually."

"Her, then. Get her up to speed just in case this goes any further. Right now, I need to get a move on. I need a shower and I'm already late."

Natalie placed a hand on my arm. "Where were you last night? I came over to ask if you wanted to share one of the dozen coffee cakes or casseroles people keep bringing by. Your lights were on, but you weren't here. Even the kids weren't around. Murphy was scratching at the door, and it was unlocked, so I let her out to go. I gave her some kibble and water, too, and locked the door behind myself."

"Thanks. Poor Murphy. Next, she'll be asking to be rehomed. Mike and I were at the hospital all night." I gave her the cliff notes version. "And Jacqui is experimenting with living at her dad's house." The pang of loss wasn't going away.

Ty grabbed my shoulder. "Is Seth going to be all right?"

I'd forgotten Ty and Seth were friends.

"He will. I just wish I had a lead on who did it. And why. If his truck had been stolen that would have made sense. Although it's possible that was the intent and when Seth came out at the wrong moment, the guy popped him, then panicked and ran. But once Seth was down . . ." I trailed off. None of this made sense. "Look, I really have to get moving. I still need to drop Mike at school and then get to work before that Neanderthal gets antsy."

"Mike can ride in with me," Ty offered. "But where is your regular partner?"

Good grief! My life had been in more turmoil than I realized. By now, I'd normally have poured out my distress over Jacqui's defection and Rafe's dad's heart attack with Natalie. I hadn't even had time to tell her about the mystery of Seth's brother Sam that I'd unearthed by accident. But the craziness of the last two days hadn't lent themselves to "girl" time.

"Rafe is on family leave. His dad had a heart attack, then surgery. It looks like he's going to be okay, but Rafe's taking time off to help his mother. I promise I'll fill you in on the zoo my life has been the last couple days when I have a few minutes to breathe. I'll send Mike over. Thanks."

I left them standing in their driveway as I hurried to my house to do my best to gird myself for what was already promising to be a grueling day and make up to my puppy for abandoning her the night before.

I let myself into the building and strode along the corridor, head down, not wishing to catch anyone's eye and get delayed.

"Deputy Quinn."

Rats. I turned to see the young detective Rafe and I had been helping with the graffiti issue hurrying after me. I curbed my impatience and waited.

"I got a lead on who might have been leaving his artwork at the church. Want to see if we can find the guy?"

Torn, I hesitated. It might be another avenue for the murder investigation, but I didn't want to leave Zack to pursue Ty without me playing anchor. "What have you got?"

"Guy at a convenience store out on King Street mentioned a homeless vet who lives out of his truck. He's apparently left examples of his talent on the store in the past. So, I have a description, but no plate number, no name, no address. Just need to go hunting."

"Okay." I bit my lip. "I need to check in with Oliver first. You on the way out?"

"I can wait. I've got a mountain of paperwork I can work on. Let me know." He saluted and turned on his heel. I watched him walk away as the wheels turned in my head.

If the graffiti artist could be found, he might turn out to be our murderer. Or be able to shed light on who else might want to do the pastor in. Won't know until we track him down, I thought as I headed to my desk and a show-down with Zack the hack.

My nemesis had made himself comfortable in my chair, further raising my hackles.

"Get out of my chair and tell me why you are so intent on pinning Price's murder on Tyler Anderson?"

Zack smirked but didn't move. "You act like he's totally innocent."

I felt like slapping the smirk off his face but managed to curb the inclination. "Because he is innocent."

Zack tipped my chair back and laced his fingers behind his head.

"And you're dead certain of this because he's a neighbor? Or a friend? Or why?"

"Because he's not that kind of person. There isn't a violent bone in that man's body."

"Really!" The chair came back to level with a jarring thud. "He's ex-Navy SEAL. Seems to me he just might have a violent bone or two or he'd never have survived the course, never mind the missions."

I didn't like to give up the height advantage standing gave me, but this discussion was overdue. I dropped into the visitor's chair opposite my desk. "That was then. This is now. Just because a man was once a lethal soldier doesn't automatically mean he can't also be a model citizen."

"Too many things just seem to be adding up."

"Coincidental things."

"And I don't believe in coincidence. Not when there are so many of them." Zack brought up a fist and propped his elbow on the desk. He lifted one finger. "Exhibit A – Anderson's wife brings explosives like those used to blow up the Church of Peace into this very building and turns them in. B – The man owns a red pickup truck that matches the description given by a neighbor who saw such a truck in the parking lot of the church the day before the graffiti was discovered. C – Anderson's son's funeral was picketed by the now dead pastor and several of his flock."

"That's not much of a motive," I tried to interrupt his litany, but he just pushed the hand toward my face and raised the pinky.

"Anderson's daughter just happens to have been in the AICE program, and involved with putting on meals for the homeless at St. Francis House which offers up another possible motive. And," he hurried on when I opened my mouth to interrupt again. "He can't recall what he ate for breakfast never mind who was with him on the day in question. Then we get a tip the murder weapon is hidden in his truck."

Zack slapped his now open palm down on the desk. "How much more *coincidence* do you expect me to swallow?"

My turn to smirk. "But you didn't find one, did you?"

"He had plenty of opportunity to move it between the time our tipster saw him put it there and we arrived to search the truck."

"Ty doesn't own a gun."

"Are you so sure his son did not?"

"Look, Zack." I took a breath and reined in my frustration. "Who is this someone who says he 'saw' Ty hide a gun in his truck? And just where was he or she when the murder went down?"

"It was a man, and he didn't leave a name. But I still think the son could have owned a few weapons even if Anderson didn't. And what about the daughter?"

"I spoke with Kiara already. She was not taken in by the pastor's charm. She knew some of the girls who were, but she wasn't. So why would her father need to avenge her?"

"Girls lie all the time when they don't want people to know how stupidly they've behaved. In this case, the daughter might want to keep it hidden so people like me wouldn't have a reason to suspect her father of foul play."

"I know Kiara. She was not lying. I'm sure she'd be willing to come in and talk with you if you need to judge her truthfulness for yourself.

Zack waved my offer away as if it didn't matter. "What about Anderson's anger issues?"

I shot from the chair; all pretense of calm discussion gone. "What are you talking about? Ty doesn't have anger issues."

Zack's smirk grew. "I heard there was a standoff at the school recently."

I gasped. The wind taken out of my sails. "What standoff?" How come I hadn't heard about this?

"One of the ladies who works in his office heard shouting behind his closed doors shortly before another man stormed out and slammed the door behind him."

"Did she say both men were shouting or just one? If she worked there, I'm sure she would have known whose voice was raised and whose was not." I couldn't wait to discuss this with Ty. Preferably without Zack along. My guess was, it hadn't been Ty slamming doors or storming out of the office, so it probably hadn't been him shouting either. And I'd never seen the man lose his temper. But he had lied to me about having an argument with someone recently if the secretary was to be believed.

Zack didn't reply right away. Maybe he already suspected Ty was not the one with temper issues. He got to his feet and brushed past me. "I'm applying for another search warrant. Chances are, if he moved it out of the truck, then he's disposed of it and we'll never find it, but I'm not ignoring the possibility it's still in his possession."

"You are so far off base." I'd be reading that warrant word for word and making sure Zack didn't turn the search into a fishing expedition for anything he might use to add flames to the bonfire he was building. "Ty is not your man and the longer you let yourself be sidetracked the longer whoever did this has to get away clean."

Zack stopped in the doorway. "Last time I checked, you don't have any other suspects."

"Paul Acosta got a lead on the graffiti artist. He asked if I wanted to go hunting with him. You're free to join us."

"I'm not clear how Acosta's case is connected, but I'll leave that to you. I don't need help applying for another warrant." He turned to leave.

"Don't—" I said halting his angry exit, but he didn't turn back. "Don't even think about executing that warrant without taking me with you."

"Whatever." Zack lifted one shoulder and disappeared. "But you better be ready to drop everything when I give you the word." His warning faded as he moved away.

I dropped into my chair, still warm from Zack's presence. But then shot to my feet, too antsy and angry to sit still. I headed for Acosta's cramped corner to interrupt his paperwork and go hunting.

CHAPTER 17

"HE'S A VETERAN. LIVING OUT OF HIS TRUCK. Doesn't seem destitute, but maybe prefers living the life," Paul Acosta informed me as he navigated through the crowded parking lot behind the sheriff's office and then past the mobile command center that had its doors open to welcome visiting law enforcement department representatives who had come to check it out.

I'd been in that mobile unit and knew St. John's County was lucky to have such an amazing asset. The deal we'd been cut to have it built to our specs more than outweighed the periodic visits by other departments considering such a pricey purchase.

"You ever worked out of that?" I asked, interrupting Paul's narrative. I had not. Not yet anyway.

He shook his head. "It's impressive, but I've never been involved when it's been deployed. But back to this graffiti guy. That neighbor you spoke to before Price got killed mentioned a red pickup truck. Right?"

I sat up straighter. "And this guy just happens to live in a red pickup?"

Paul grinned at me. "And he's got a beef against the Church of Peace and it's leader."

"How did you—"

My question was interrupted by the ringing of my phone, a ring tone I'd just recently assigned to Seth. I held up a finger and answered.

"Hope I'm not disturbing important detective work." There was a hint of laughter in Seth's voice. A good sign.

"You sound better."

"I am. They're letting me out later today. I hope it's okay. I asked Mike to pick me up."

"I bet he's thrilled at the chance to drive your truck, but that truck isn't in your driveway. At least, not yet."

"Where is it, then? Still at the Habitat project?"

"No, they brought it here to dust it for prints and hoping to find something to send them in the right direction for catching whoever attacked you."

"Oh. Well. I guess it will have to be an Uber then."

"Look, give me a call when they're ready to discharge you. If there's a possibility I can get away, I'll come after you. You remember anything more about what happened?"

Seth made a frustrated sighing sound.

"Don't push it. It will come back," I hurried to assure him. "Has anyone been in to get your statement? As much as you do recall anyway?"

"Yup. Nice kid. Said to call him Mac."

"He's not exactly a kid." I chuckled. Rob McKenzie's path had been intersecting with mine repeatedly recently. No longer a rookie, and standing six feet ten inches in stocking feet, he towered over me. I'd come to respect his apparently natural aptitude for police work. He had the instincts of someone who'd been on the job a lot longer.

As Seth asked about getting his truck back, something clicked in my mind. I tried to grasp the thought and missed Seth's next comment."

"What?"

"I asked if you wanted to join me for pizza tonight. With Mike, of course."

"Shouldn't you be taking it easy?"

"I figured I'd order it and have you pick it up. No effort on my part at all."

My shoulders relaxed. An evening spent with Seth would be nice, and I had no problem with picking up dinner on my way.

"Sounds like a plan, but right now I need to let you go. I'll touch base later to confirm. And I'll ask about your truck."

Seth made a kissing sound. Even though there was no way Paul could have overheard, heat flowed into my cheeks. "Same to you," I responded before clicking off.

Paul glanced across the cruiser at me, eyebrows lifted. I prayed the flush wasn't as bright as it felt. "So, this guy with the truck," he said, ending my battle with embarrassment. "I was talking to the clerk at Ken's on King Street. He said this guy comes in to buy a sandwich every afternoon. If we go hang out and wait, we might catch him."

I glanced at the clock on the dash. "Any specific time?"

Paul shrugged. "Varies. The kid thinks he might even park there overnight, but he's not on that shift so he wasn't sure. If we don't see the guy this afternoon, I plan to come back tonight and wait. But you don't have to wait with me. Sounds like you have other plans."

I considered the options. Lurking in Paul's cruiser praying I didn't have to pee before our guy showed up as opposed to curled up with my shoes off eating pizza with Seth. "Did the clerk you spoke with give you the impression this guy was someone to be wary of?"

"Nope. Said the guy hangs out to chat sometimes. Seems friendly enough. I'm fine with doing the stakeout on my own."

As he said this, we pulled into Ken's Corner Store parking lot. Empty of any vehicle other than our own, we climbed out and studied the area.

"Let's go talk to them," I nodded towards two raggedly dressed individuals sitting in a sunny patch against the fence facing North Velusia.

Paul followed me as I headed across the empty lot. As we rounded a fence littered with empty drink cups, bits of sandwich wrappers and other detritus the wind had blown up against it, the vagrants looked up. The young woman barely looked old enough to be into her twenties if that. Her stringy blond hair was mostly hidden under the hoodie she wore. A black male about the same age, got to his feet, a look of wary alarm on his face. I guess even without uniforms we looked like cops.

I held out my hand, palm down. "We're not here to hassle you. Just wanted to ask a couple questions."

The woman lowered her head again, hair and hoodie sliding down to hide her face completely. The man squared his shoulders. "Like what kind of questions?"

"Like if you've ever seen a gentleman around here who lives out of a red pickup truck."

The man shrugged. "Maybe."

"Have you seen him recently?"

Again, the shrug.

"Do you know his name?" Paul asked, picking up the questioning.

"Dusty. 'S-all I know. He's an older dude. Doesn't mix much with our crowd."

"What crowd does he mix with?" Paul persisted.

"Mostly vets."

I jumped back into the conversation. "You have any names?"

"That's all I'm saying. C'mon Selena. Let's split." He tugged on the girl's sweatshirt, and she scrambled to her feet.

With furtive glances over their shoulders, they hustled across the street, barely missing a motorist who'd just gotten a break in the traffic headed downtown.

"I'm pretty sure I can find them again if we want to harass them some more," Paul said.

"You've seen them before?"

"Yeah. I was on patrol out here before they moved me over to detective. They live at the homeless camp by the tracks." He nodded toward the trees on the far side of King Street. "I got called out there a few times. This couple never gave anyone trouble that I know of, though."

"Dusty," I muttered as we retraced our steps to the convenience store. "Did you ever meet anyone called Dusty when you were out there?"

Paul shook his head. "Nope. Maybe he just likes Ken's sandwiches and hangs somewhere else most of the time. Besides, no way he'd leave a truck untended for very long and he couldn't get it out to the camp since there's no road. I'm going in for a cup of coffee. You up for one?"

"Always up for coffee. I'll keep watch."

While Paul headed for the store, I rested my butt against the fender of his ride and perused my email, a half an eye on traffic. Two cars pulled in and parked in front of the store, but neither were red or pickups.

Halfway through an irritating email full of demands from my lieutenant, a flash of red caught my eye.

The red pickup truck did not turn into the lot but continued west. I squinted trying to make out the license plate, but it was more than half obscured with dirt. I only got the first letter and the last two digits. Would take some digging to get a match.

Approaching me with coffee in each hand, Paul glanced over his shoulder toward where my gaze was fixed. "See something?"

"A red pickup. Have you any idea how many red pickup trucks there are in this county? I only caught a partial."

We settled into Paul's vehicle, and he woke up his laptop, fed in the letter and numbers I'd seen, then sat back to sip his coffee.

"I'm not sure this is our guy," Paul said.

"And yet, here we sit." I took a tentative sip of my coffee and found it remarkably good. "At least the coffee is excellent."

"There is that. But this guy… Dusty. The clerk I just spoke with never mentioned a name, but the way he describes him, he doesn't sound like a violent individual. Just a graffiti artist of some talent, who likes to live off the grid and make all his political statements with artwork." Paul put the cruiser in gear. "And he was in earlier. Not likely to be back again today unless he's parked out here after closing."

My mind still worked on the hint of a hint that flashed into my head an hour earlier when my phone rang, cutting off whatever thought I was pursuing.

"I've got the warrant and I'll give you exactly ten minutes before I'm on my way," Zack said without fanfare.

I glanced at our location. "Fifteen and you better be waiting." I hung up before he could object.

CHAPTER 18

AS I CLIMBED into Zack's unmarked car while he impatiently drummed his thumbs on the steering wheel, the hint of a hint that had been nagging at me suddenly clarified itself.

"The graffiti artist drives a red pickup truck."

Zack turned an irritated expression on me. "And that should be important to me because...?"

"Just because Ty drives one does not mean he's your guy. He's no artist, but my information suggests this graffiti artist might be the person who defiled the Church of Peace. What if he returned to the scene and was confronted by Pastor Price?"

Zack's frown suggested he hadn't taken any interest in the whole graffiti issue Paul Acosta had been working on or any connection it might have to the pastor's death.

"You've talked to this guy?"

"Paul and I were hunting him down when you called."

Zack's condescending sigh put my back up.

I matched his sigh, lacing mine with as much contempt as I could muster. "That guy we took to the hospital last night? He's a friend of mine and he also drives a red pickup." Another random itch just clicked. Both Ty and Seth were involved with the Habitat projects. What if the killer decided to plant the murder weapon on Ty to deflect blame, and thought Seth's truck was Ty's? Only Seth surprised him and got clocked for it.

Zack's tongue pressed the side of his cheek outward as he glanced across at me. "You pointing a finger at Cameron, instead?"

I clenched my fists in frustration. "I'm saying neither of them did it, but maybe someone wanted it to look like Ty did." Which, of course, made it highly unlikely the graffiti artist was also our killer. No way would he direct attention to a vehicle that matched his own. I paused in my argument with Zack to send Paul a text with this thought.

"Everything you have against Ty Anderson is circumstantial. You're making me wonder if you have something against the color of his skin. Are you a racist?" I spit out the question like it tasted bad, which it did. Racism didn't belong in police work. Didn't belong anywhere.

Zack slanted a brief glance my way but didn't respond.

Disgust seeped into my chest. "I don't like you much, and that's not exactly a secret, but I thought you were above that."

"I. Am. Not. Racist." Zack kept his eyes on the road, his lower jaw thrust forward.

"Then why are you so anxious to pin this on Ty?"

"He's our best suspect. Our only suspect."

"The only one on your radar you mean." Apparently, Zack would rather pin the murder on an innocent man than do the work to dig out the truth. I wanted to ask if he was really that lazy, but I bit my tongue before letting the acid out.

Four exhausting hours later, Zack finally admitted defeat and left, a very unhappy man. It wasn't until after I'd hugged Ty and Natalie, assuring them I was working hard to find the real culprit and thus take the heat off them, that I remembered I'd arrived with Zack and my ride was at Central. Ty offered to drive me up.

"Let me make a couple calls first," I said stepping out onto their veranda. "I'll let you know if I still need a ride."

I started with Paul, but he had nothing new to report. Then I called Mike to see where he was and if he needed a ride from wherever that was.

"I'll come get you, Mom."

"In what vehicle?" His Camaro was still in the garage across the lawn as far as I knew.

There was some whispering I couldn't make out. Then Mike was back.

"In Seth's truck. I'm over at Seth's and some guy dropped it off here about an hour ago. Seth said I could come get you." Excitement filled his offer.

"Okay, but please. Please. Drive carefully."

"I always drive carefully." He hung up before I could respond.

I prayed his claim was truthful. I'd seen too many crashes involving youthful drivers who probably told their parents they were careful drivers.

I knocked, then stuck my head in the door to let Ty know I was not going to need a ride after all. Then filled the waiting time by checking my always overfull inbox of email.

Pleased as punch to be the designated driver for a change, and driving Seth's monstrous red beast, Mike arrived a few minutes later and gushed about the truck all the way to central.

"I thought you were pretty pleased with the Camaro," I'd said when he let me get a word in edgewise.

His grin widened. "I love my Camaro, but this truck is awesome."

As I climbed down from Seth's truck and cautioned my son to drive carefully one more time, he rolled his eyes. "Mo-om!"

"Just let me be a mother for a minute here," I responded, blowing him a kiss. "See you back at Seth's."

"Don't forget the pizza," he said, rolling down the window to remind me. "I'll collect Murphy on my way, so you won't have to worry about walking her before we eat."

He waited like a gentleman while I unlocked my car and climbed in, then carefully backed out of his slot and headed back toward Route 1. Mike really was a good kid. Somewhere along the line, I'd done a few things right, even if my current relationship with my daughter was on rocky ground.

What was Jacqui doing right now? I wondered as I followed Mike out onto Route 1. Part of me wanted her to be missing me, but the other part prayed she was happy and settling in. Perhaps our relationship would be less strained when she was back on my turf for weekends and holidays. I ached with the conflict of missing her and wanting whatever was best for her.

As I pulled into a vacant spot in front of Tony's to collect Seth's pizza order, I realized thoughts of Jacqui had filled my head to the exclusion of Zack and my frustration with him for the entire drive. Maybe there was hope for a restful, pleasant evening with Seth and Mike.

Mike was standing by the back door of Seth's truck talking to someone I couldn't see as I parked and grabbed the pizza boxes.

"Who are you talking to?" I asked, rounding the bed of the truck.

"Murphy," Mike replied. "She's got her head stuck under the seat trying to pull something out and she won't let me help."

I handed Mike the pizza boxes and called my puppy. "Murphy, come."

The puppy's butt swayed as she wagged her tail, but she didn't come.

"C'mon, Murph. Whatever's under there can't be as good as hot pizza." I reached for her collar and tugged.

Her head popped out as if noticing my presence for the first time. The wagging intensified, but before I could get a better hold on her, she shoved her nose back under the seat and growled.

What the hell was under that seat? Good God, what if it's a snake? My heart jolted at the possibility.

"Murphy!" I commanded in my sternest tone.

With one last muffled woof, she backed out and sat staring at the space beneath the driver's seat.

Mike slipped her leash into my hand, and I snapped it onto her collar. "Off." I pointed toward the ground.

Reluctantly, the puppy jumped down from the truck and began dancing around my legs eager for my approval. I ruffled the silky fur behind her ears and told her she was good. Then I handed the leash to my son and went back to my car. No way was I going to confront whatever was under that seat without me seeing it first.

Flashlight in hand, I bent and aimed the beam under the seat.

Nothing. I aimed the beam higher hoping I wasn't going to see two slanted eyes glaring back at me from the coils beneath the seat. Just a piece of an old cleaning rag. That wasn't like Seth. I reached to pull it free, but it was firmly caught in the springs. No wonder Murphy couldn't get it loose. I tugged harder, heard a ripping sound, and almost tumbled onto my ass as the rag came free. With a clatter!

Cloth doesn't clatter!

With what I now saw was an oil-stained t-shirt in one hand, I aimed the flashlight back under the seat again.

"Son of a bitch!" How had they missed this at Central? The deputy going over Seth's truck must have been in a hurry, dusted for prints and called it a day.

"What is it?" Mike asked, pizza boxes still balanced in one hand and the puppy eagerly pulling at the leash in the other.

Without answering, I pulled out my phone and hit Zack's contact.

"I thought you said you were done for the night," the man answered without a greeting.

"I think I might have found our murder weapon."

"Where are you?" All annoyance had fled.

I gave him Seth's address and he curtly replied that he was on the way.

"Take the pizza and Murphy in. Apologize to Seth and tell him I'll be in as soon as I take care of this little detail."

Mike glanced at the house, then back at me. "How do you know it's not Seth's?"

"Because he doesn't own a handgun."

"You think this had anything to do with Seth getting whacked over the head last night?"

I thought it had everything to do with Seth getting knocked unconscious, but the thought that my son had been that close to a man who'd likely committed murder had my guts in a twist. "Maybe," I muttered. "But, please, just go inside. I'll be in as soon as Deputy Oliver gets here and takes possession of it. You can ask Seth if he knows anything about it. Text me immediately if he says yes."

Mike nodded and turned toward the house.

Clearly Zack had been on this side of the old city and likely broke every speed law considering he blew into Seth's driveway and stopped with a rattle of gravel just a few minutes after the door shut behind my son and seconds after the text confirming that Seth knew nothing about the gun, or the shirt appeared on my phone.

"Where is it?" Zack said, striding across the lawn.

I pointed toward the truck. "In the wrong red pickup truck. Kind of confirms my earlier assumption that whoever did the killing is trying to misdirect us, got the wrong truck and the wrong fall guy. It's under the driver's seat."

"You touch it?"

I hissed my disgust at his opinion of my intelligence. "No one has touched it except maybe my dog. Watch out for slobber. It was wrapped in this." I handed him the shirt, which I noticed belatedly, had a Florida Gator on it. That wasn't Seth or Ty's alma mater.

Zack squatted down, peered under the seat, and grunted. I handed him my flashlight.

Aiming the beam under the seat, he swore. Then pulled a pen from his pocket and fished the weapon out with the pen thrust through the trigger guard. He held it up and inspected it. Then stood.

"This your boyfriend's truck?"

"Yes, and he has an alibi for the day of the murder. He was at school tutoring kids with special needs. Also, neither the shirt, nor the gun are his. And, in the spirit of full disclosure, this car was at Central being dusted for prints earlier today. Seth was working on a Habitat project yesterday and he was the last to leave. When he carried his tools out to the truck, someone struck him with something hard and knocked him unconscious. I'm betting it was whoever stashed that gun up under his seat."

"He see who it was?"

"If he had, I'd have told you this morning. But he didn't. You can read Rob McKenzie's report for the details. He was the responding deputy."

Without further comment, Zack shook open the lid of a slender cardboard evidence box, dropped the gun into it, and fastened the zip-ties. He dropped the shirt into a paper sack and added it to his hoard. "Hopefully there will be prints we can use. And maybe some DNA on the shirt."

"I'm leaving you with the processing and paperwork since you were so eager to find it. Like I said, the truck was already dusted for prints so you can look the results of that up, too." I turned and headed for the house. "See you tomorrow," I tossed back over my shoulder.

Maybe by then Zack would have a name. It would be nice if the weapon had been registered, but I wasn't holding out hope. Maybe Paul Acosta would have caught up with the graffiti artist. And maybe we could close the case. But for tonight . . .

I relaxed my shoulders and sighed. A pleasant evening with Seth and without Zack awaited me.

CHAPTER 19

MY BODY SAGGED AGAINST the soft leather upholstery of Seth's oversized couch, my mind flitting from one facet of my troubling case to another against the background of men's voices as Seth guided Mike through lessons on a flight simulation program. I'm off the clock, I reminded myself and forced my mind elsewhere. My gaze strayed to the floor to ceiling bookshelves to my right. More specifically to what looked suspiciously like the scrapbook Seth had taken from me on my last visit bookended by a collection of high school yearbooks.

The mystery of his missing brother Sam, and Seth's steadfast belief that Sam was still out there somewhere. What had driven him all these years in the face of everyone else giving up?

The couch beside me sagged. Seth's arm slinked along the back, then reeled me in against his side.

"Should I ask?" he murmured in my ear.

I let my head drop against his shoulder, letting weariness take over. "I was thinking about Sam."

The big body next to me stiffened, making me regret my candor, but he didn't remove his arm or free himself of my closeness. Mike continued to drive his artificial airplane, in a whole other world from the one Seth and I inhabited. Just when I decided Seth wasn't going to acknowledge my comment, he spoke up.

"He loved me, and I've never been able to shake the feeling he's been counting on me to find him."

I tipped my head back to gaze up at Seth's strong profile, the light of the flight simulation video flickering across the clean angles of cheekbone and forehead. "But you were just a toddler when . . ." I hesitated.

"But I remember."

I straightened and looked into Seth's face. "Are you sure it's not a combination of things people have said about him that you remember?"

Again, he hesitated, perhaps wondering if he should just tell me to drop the subject or change it himself. "It's *my* memory. My dad only confirmed it."

Thinking maybe he'd share it if I wasn't staring him down, I settled back into his embrace.

"He was seven or eight." Seth's words ruffled the loose strands of hair on my temple. "I was maybe two or three. We still lived in the apartment over the bar. My mom was active at our church and every week she'd be out at some meeting or another. Usually we had a babysitter, but sometimes my dad would bring us downstairs while he worked. The cops that hung out there didn't seem to mind Sam and me pestering them for attention and we usually scored a candy bar or someone's dessert. But eventually I'd get tired. Sam would sit in a quiet corner and let me curl up into his lap and fall asleep."

Seth stopped speaking and I thought that was all he was planning to share, but then he went on. "That part my dad told me. What I remember vividly is looking up at Sam in the dim light. Looking into his dark brown eyes as he sang songs to me. His eyes looked like love." Seth broke off again, as if the memory was too intimate or too sentimental to put into words.

I kept my mouth shut, not wanting to interrupt the memory.

When next he spoke, his voice was so soft I could barely hear the words over the sound of Mike's flight simulation game. "I see his eyes in the mirror when I shave. Except they're mine. But still, I see his. Sometimes I imagine I can feel his arms around me. Sometimes I even hear his voice." Seth shook his head. "Of course, by now his voice will be that of a man, not the boy I hear in my head."

When Seth didn't continue, I dared to ask. "How do you know it's a memory and not just a vision you conjured up because you were desperate to remember a brother who was gone?"

"I told my dad about it once, years afterward. He was flabbergasted. Because I was only a toddler. Dad didn't think I could possibly remember that far back, but no one else except the three of us knew about those nights. Well, some of the cops that hung out there would remember, but it was unlikely any of them would have talked to me about it. Not after Sam disappeared, anyway. So, it wasn't something anyone told me. And it wasn't just the product of a fairy tale because it really happened. My dad remembered watching Sam cradle me in his lap while I fell asleep."

Astonishment filled me, like it must have filled Seth's dad. For a toddler to recall such a poignant experience with such accuracy seemed nothing short of amazing.

"And how does that memory convince you Sam is still living?"

Seth tapped his chest. "Because I'd feel it here if he wasn't." Such certainty in his words. Had I ever been that certain about anything with so little to trust in?

"Tell me about your search to find him."

Seth tucked his lower lip in beneath his upper teeth, then slowly let it return to its usual place. With a grunt, he pushed himself sideways and reached for the scrapbook. "Take it home with you and read it at your leisure." He said, placing it in my lap. Then he put his thumb and forefinger under my chin, tipped my head up to his and kissed me, ending the conversation.

If it hadn't been for Mike sitting just feet away, there's no telling where that kiss would have led. If Seth had asked me to stay, I'd have been sorely tempted, despite my son and the good example I wanted to set. But eventually, worn out from my day, I'd disentangled myself from the comfortable embrace and gotten to my feet to collect my son and head home to our own beds.

This morning, after I'd dropped Mike off at school and stopped for a cup of coffee, I sat in the DOS Coffee Shop parking lot, sipping the steamy brew, and poking through Seth's notebook again. I'd stayed up far longer than I should have the night before, unwilling to put it down once I'd gotten started.

It began with the clippings from local newspapers in the Wilmington, North Carolina area that I'd scanned before. Large ones with interviews and conjectures at the start, petering out to single column updates, spread over longer and longer periods of time.

What had kept me up and reading long after the light should have been out were things in Sam's boyish handwriting. School assignments, letters to Santa – God only knew where they'd been unearthed, and a tale about a very small boy written on lined paper with the heading: For Seth.

It was a collection of short stories. Stories about a very small boy and the amazing adventures he'd gotten up to. Sam had quite an imagination for a kid of seven or eight. I wondered if he'd read them to Seth after they'd been written or if he'd made them up for Seth, then written them down afterward.

The stories were followed by a collection of sympathy cards and letters from friends and relatives, all holding out hope and offering prayers, but those had dribbled in at longer and longer intervals like the newspaper updates.

Several pages of photos came next. Photos of Sam; alone, with family, posed for school pictures, playing sports and several with a toddler that I knew without asking was Seth.

The last pages were all notes in Seth's handwriting. At least I assumed it was all his. I recognized his adult style, but the earliest pages must have been written before he even got to high school.

Those early entries were filled with the outpouring of heartache from a little boy waiting for news that never came. As the handwriting grew into Seth's sturdy adult style, the notes were more factual, less emotional, but no less certain. There were notes about Seth's searches. Online mostly, but also letters written to various authorities followed by typed or printed email replies. Most were attempts to locate or identify the unknown woman who'd been dressed as hospital staff who had reportedly sat with Sam when he'd been brought into the ER by the EMTs after the fire at their small upstairs apartment. But she had disappeared as completely as the young boy, leaving not a trace of her identity or destination.

Sam was nine at the time. Old enough to remember who he was, who his parents were and where he lived, so if he'd survived, why had he made no effort to get home?

I took another swig of coffee and found my travel mug empty. How long had I been here contemplating a 37-year-old cold case when Zack the Hack was surely at work pursuing our present-day case that needed solving?

"Dustin Labelle," Acosta announced striding into my office not five minutes after I'd arrived and pulled open the file on Pastor Price.

"Who's Dustin Labelle?"

"The graffiti artist and right as we speak, he's sitting at a table outside Panera. Let's go before he disappears."

I scrambled to scoop up my gear and hurry after Acosta's retreating form.

The young detective didn't break any speed laws, but hopefully we had managed to arrive before our quarry had moved on.

The only customer currently seated at the outside tables appeared to be middle-aged, lanky, tall, dressed in worn blue jeans which was the description Acosta had been given. The surfer's tan and dreads also fit. Looked like we'd found our man. Judging by his slouched posture as we approached, he wasn't inclined to make a run for it. His eyes narrowed, but he calmly continued eating.

"Are you Dustin Labelle?" Acosta asked, taking a seat opposite the man, uninvited.

"Might be," the man replied, then shoved the last of his sandwich into his mouth and chewed.

I grabbed a chair from the next table over and joined them. "I understand you are a man of some talent, Mr. Labelle."

"I like to think so. But please call me Dusty. Everyone does."

"Have you been decorating the Church of Peace lately?" Acosta asked, getting to the point.

Dusty's brows rose, but he didn't respond.

"If it was your work, I'm impressed," I said, hoping to appeal to his vanity.

"Am I under arrest?" He wiped his mouth and set the napkin in the empty paper tray.

"No one's pressing charges for the artwork," Acosta told him.

The shoulders that had been tense a moment before relaxed. "Then why are you here harassing me?" He looked around as if he might have missed part of his meal.

"So, the boots and helmet were your work?" I pressed.

"Might have been."

"Why?" Acosta persisted.

"Why not?" Dusty replied with a snicker. "The man's a prick."

"Were the genitals yours, as well?" My curiosity got the better of me.

"Maybe." Dusty wasn't eager to confess even though Acosta had already told him no charges were being pressed for the graffiti. If he was in any way connected to the killing, he was a very cool customer, but as we sat there discussing his work, I got the gut feeling he was not connected with the Pastor's demise.

"Want to tell us why?" Acosta asked.

"Why the artwork?" Dusty scratched his head. "You ever meet the guy?"

"Actually, yes," Acosta agreed. "Several times."

"A piece of work, right?"

I saw Acosta's hand slip to the butt of his gun. "Did you kill him?"

Dusty's feet slid off the chair rung and slammed onto the concrete patio. "Good God, no! Why would I want to do that?"

"Because he was a prick, I think you said." Acosta smirked.

"I was having too much fun taunting him with reminders of just how ungodly a human he was. How did he die? Blown up in that explosion I heard about?"

"Something like that," I finally joined the conversation. "So where were you three nights ago. The night after the boots and helmet artwork?"

Dusty scratched his head again. Either it was a nervous habit, or he had lice.

He squinted as if thinking. Then brightened. "At the Amphitheater. Watching The Bare Naked Ladies."

"Can anyone vouch for that?"

"Yeah. One of their road crew is a friend of mine. He's the guy that got me into the place. I was there all afternoon, visiting with the crew. Then I stayed for the show and partied some more afterward."

"And when did you leave?" It was going to be pretty air-tight if he was telling the truth. I hated to give up on the only promising lead we had.

"Got kicked out. Ask the cops from the beach." Dusty stood up. "I got hammered and fell asleep in my truck. They found me there the next morning and suggested I leave before they found a reason to arrest me. That all?"

Acosta and I got to our feet as well. "That's all for now."

"But no one is pressing charges for the artwork, right?" Dusty was doing his best to appear unconcerned, but clearly wanted to be anywhere else but under our scrutiny.

"Price never changed his mind about that, but he's dead now so unless someone else decides to, you're good to go. Just don't leave town."

Dusty didn't wait for a second invitation to be gone from our presence.

"How are we going to find him again?" I asked as Dusty disappeared around the building. "It's not like he has an address or anything."

Acosta grinned. "But he's got a cell phone we can ping."

CHAPTER 20

JUST BEFORE I LEFT CENTRAL after an afternoon of catching up on paperwork and getting nowhere with the Price investigation, Sgt. Broussard strode into my cramped little office and lowered himself into my guest chair with a sigh.

"You're going to have to play nice and try to find some middle ground."

"There is no middle ground with Deputy Oliver," I responded not bothering to pretend I didn't know what he was getting at. "He's so determined to wrap this up in a neat little bow and move on that he's dogging an innocent man."

"Ty Anderson is a person of interest. You can't ignore that reality," Broussard said, as he relaxed into the chair. Then he sat forward again, an urgent expression furrowing his brow. "Rafe Morgan called."

At the sound of my partner's name, my heart lurched. The one call I'd managed to connect with him, Rafe had been optimistic. Serious surgery but his dad was on the mend.

"His father passed away this morning. Rafe asked for a month's leave. He's got the time coming and he wants to be there for his mother."

"Holy hell. I thought his dad was recovering."

"Things went sideways. He had trouble getting off the ventilator. A lifetime of smoking to thank for that," Broussard opined.

"Poor Rafe. He was so optimistic when I talked to him. But I'm not surprised about the time off. He said he was going to take some

133

even before this." He'd already been worrying about his mom and how she was going to cope with an invalid. Now there would be a funeral to plan.

"Which means," Broussard made a clucking sound with his tongue. "You and Zack Oliver will be working together for a while longer."

My heart fell. Bad enough Rafe was dealing with his dad's death, and I was dealing with my daughter's defection, but now I had to work with Zack for another month.

"There's something you should know about Oliver. Might help put his rush to nail Anderson into perspective for you."

I started to protest but Broussard held up a hand. "Hear me out before you start objecting."

I sat back and folded my hands in my lap. Patience wasn't one of my virtues.

"A couple years ago, Oliver was on a case with a lot of similarities to this one. A series of circumstantial things pointed at one person of interest, but Oliver kept holding back, wanting to find something more solid. Something that no one could misinterpret. He was working alone at the time so there was no partner to bounce things off. Oliver looked at every single person that was even remotely connected, two of whom had very good reasons to do the woman in. She was a piece of work herself with several people who might want her gone. Oliver hesitated over the one person of interest with more circumstantial connections but without any obvious reason to kill her.

"Might have had something to do with the suspect being a woman. A well-spoken woman; educated, personable and well-liked by all her colleagues. She just didn't seem like the type. So, Oliver held off, looking for more conclusive proof. The DA didn't help. He wasn't eager to have the detective on the case arresting a woman with connections to people in high places and giving the department a bad name."

"But the woman was the guilty party?" I asked, my interest caught.

"Guilty as sin," Broussard confirmed. "But before that was determined, she'd killed three more people.

"It was a case of a lover's triangle. A very messy triangle. The first killing had been a co-worker who happened to have been having an affair with a married man with a couple kids. The woman who did the killing was the last person to have seen her alive, and they'd had an argument earlier in the day. And her alibi was that she'd been out running on the beach at the time of the killing.

"When the autopsy showed the dead woman to be pregnant, the lover seemed a more likely suspect. Except, his wife insisted he'd been at his son's birthday party at the time of the killing.

"Then it was discovered that the connected, respected woman, had also been in a relationship with the same guy but had managed to keep it off everyone's radar. She had to have known about the wife all along but apparently the discovery of a third woman and that woman's pregnancy was the tipping point. The guy broke it off with her and planned to leave his wife so he could be with the third woman and their expected baby."

"She killed the competition. And who else?" I prayed it wasn't the wife or kids."

"The lover, the lover's wife and one of his kids; a thirteen-year-old boy who had tried to protect his mother. The daughter just happened to be at a sleep-over, but the impact of losing her entire family was traumatic. Oliver blamed himself for the deaths of the wife and son, and especially what that little girl had to live through."

I slumped into my chair. Broussard's story explained a lot about Zack's determination now. Also said a lot about Zack that I'd never considered before. He always just came off as arrogant and self-assured. Like he was never wrong. I was definitely going to have to adjust my attitude toward the man.

Broussard got to his feet and headed for the door. "Tomorrow, I want the three of us to sit down and go over what we know and what we don't know and determine where to go next on this one. Okay?" He hovered in the doorway, waiting for my response.

"Got it, boss. When do you want me here?"

"Nine. And ready to listen to all sides of the issue. With an open mind." Then he was gone.

I was very subdued when I let myself into my empty echoing house a short time later. My heart was heavy with the news of Rafe's dad, and the empty house did nothing to lift my spirits. Mike had returned to Seth's, to help the invalid out. Seth would probably have a cow at being called an invalid, but he was supposed to be taking it easy for a few more days. Mike had offered to stay and help out and had apparently decided Murphy should go along for company.

I headed for my room to change into running gear. Then I stopped at Jacqui's door.

For the first time in memory, her room was tidy. The bed neatly made. No clothes strewn about. No books or school paraphernalia scattered across her desk. The most telling thing was the missing laptop.

Jacqui was living with her dad. I slumped onto the edge of her bed, overwhelmed. I felt like crying.

Despite having no kids to wake and send off to school, and no dog to feed and walk, I was the last to take a seat in the small conference room where Broussard had the contents of a file spread out in front of him. A carafe of steaming coffee with one remaining mug with the SJSD logo sitting in the center of the table. Paul Acosta and Zack Oliver glanced up briefly, and Acosta nodded a greeting. Zack waved two fingers at me in some sort of acknowledgment. Both turned back to Broussard.

"Glad you could join us," the Sergeant said in a neutral voice. I wasn't late, but I supposed I could have made a better effort to be early. Broussard shuffled a small stack of reports that looked like the graffiti complaints.

"Paul has filled us in on your interview yesterday with William LaBelle, and he's quite certain that the graffiti is not connected with the death of Pastor Price. You concur?"

"I wanted to like him for it, but we checked his alibi and he's off the list," I admitted, as I reached for the coffee and poured myself a cup.

"Are you onboard with that?" Broussard looked at Acosta.

"Yeah. Dusty admitted to all the artwork and since he can't be the doer of either the church demolition or the shooting of the pastor, I think that closes that book." As if in emphasis, Acosta swiped the file closed on his tablet.

"Anything else you can think of to add to the investigation of the pastor's death? Anything you might have learned from the people you spoke with over the last few weeks?"

Acosta shook his head, then stopped abruptly with a finger in the air. "There was the guy on the fire squad that responded to the explosion. He was on a rant about it all being 'just deserts.' Anyone checked into him?"

"You got a name?" Zack asked, stylus poised over his own tablet.

"Yeah, Cambridge. Ed Cambridge. I didn't hear everything. It was crazy and there was a lot of shouting, but Cambridge said something along the lines of men who defile young women deserve what they get. Don't know if he had personal knowledge or if he was just repeating something others said. A few weeks ago, when I responded to the penis graffiti, one of Price's parishioners said Pastor Price was estranged from his own brother after he'd seduced the brother's fiancée."

"Have we talked to the brother yet?" Broussard asked looking from Zack to me.

"Not," Zack answered.

"Thanks for that info, Acosta. We should be talking to Ed Cambridge, too."

I scribbled quickly in my reliable old pencil and paper notebook, happy to have two new avenues of investigation to pursue. "My informant suggested there might be several women Price has lured into a relationship, then dumped. I've questioned a couple of them."

"And they all seem to be part of a club for smart kids at school that one of Ty Anderson's daughters belonged to," Zack was quick to note.

"Who else have we looked at. Besides Ms. Anderson?"

"We ruled out the families of two other soldiers whose funerals were recently picketed by Price and his followers," Zack offered, ignoring the issue of defiled young women.

"In reference to Price's sexual exploits," Broussard asked pointedly.

"I spoke to two women." I flipped back a few pages. My source gave me the name of her niece as one of the girls in this club and I spoke to her. She was otherwise occupied at the time. Likewise, Ty's daughter who now lives in New York, since she was home for her brother's funeral. Kiara also claims she was never one of Price's conquests. She spurned his advances, after which he called her an 'uppity black bitch.' Apparently, Price was something of a bigot as well."

"Were you going to name this other woman?" Zack asked pointedly.

"I'd rather not. Rafe and I discussed it, and we both agreed no one in her family knew about it other than the aunt and that's where it needs to stop."

"Maybe I should be the judge of that," Broussard said, the tilt of his head telling me he wasn't pleased with my withholding information.

"The young woman involved is now in college. It's been several years since she was on the receiving end of Price's attentions. And she, too, was smart enough to see through the charm and turn him down." At Broussard's clamped jaw, I sighed. "Okay, but it stays right here in this room. I promised Madison. Her father is Deputy Devers and she talked to her aunt because she knew what her dad would do if he ever found out that a pervert had propositioned his daughter. And from all I've learned, Devers never did find out. As for alibis, Devers was at a meeting in Orlando at the time of the church fire and Price's death. So, it can stop right here. He doesn't need to ever know unless his daughter chooses to tell him."

Broussard nodded. "Fair enough. But what about the other young women that you know of?"

"There's one possibility I haven't been able to track down yet," I admitted. "Actually two. Rafe and I were sent to cover the death of a young woman before this business with Price and the church came up.

It was an open and shut case of suicide, but now that I think about it, the family were members of Price's parish. And she was also a member of AICE. That smart kids' group at school."

"Add the parents to the list to check for alibis," Broussard said. "And who is this possibility you haven't checked into yet?"

I slid the sonogram from my notebook and pushed it across the desk to Broussard. Zack started to intercept it but thought better of the urge.

"T. Willis," Broussard said studying the image. "And this is connected to Price, how?"

"I found it in his desk at the church."

Zack started to his feet but fell back into his chair at a glare from Broussard.

Broussard studied the image for a moment longer, then handed it to Zack, whose eyebrows rose when he realized what the paper was. "Humph," was all he said as he returned the paper to Broussard after showing it to Acosta. Now all three were staring at me, waiting for an explanation.

"The crime scene team had already been through everything," I defended myself and my having withheld the knowledge until now. "I asked both Madison Devers and Kiara Anderson if they knew anyone named T. Willis, but neither did. I think they were enough ahead in school of whoever this woman is they never crossed paths. But—" I broke off abruptly as memory of Seth's 'Sam Cameron' notebook shelved in a row of yearbooks came to mind. "But I think I know where to look next."

Broussard gave his head a slight shake and clipped the sonogram to the cover of the case file. "And where is that?

"Yearbooks," I said, sitting back in my chair, pleased to have come up with the solution.

"Good thought," Broussard nodded. "We should also be talking to whoever is in charge of AICE and see if they can shed any light on any of this."

Zack nodded. I scribbled in my notebook.

"What about the gun my dog found in Seth Cameron's truck? Has that been processed yet?"

Zack grimaced. "Yeah. I put a rush on it. It is the murder weapon, but no prints. Numbers filed off and the shooter was careful to wipe every part of it down. Even the shirt was a dead end. It was old, but clean. Nothing to be learned from that either."

"Except that it was a Gator's shirt, and the car driven by the guy who rang Cameron's bell had a Gator's plate according to my son. Can't ignore there's a possible connection."

"To whom? A few thousand graduates of The University of Florida?"

I sagged back into my chair. It was a slim hope at best anyway. "Like all the red pickup trucks in the county," I tossed back at Zack who was always quick to point out that Ty drove just such a truck.

"I asked you to play nice," Broussard reminded us with a frown.

"It seems to me that someone is trying to point a finger in Ty Anderson's direction," I reminded my boss. "Why else would the murder weapon be planted in a red pickup truck parked at a Habitat site and an anonymous tip called in sending Zack off on a wild chase searching for the murder weapon in the wrong man's truck?"

"Allegedly wrong man's truck," Zack corrected me.

I glared at him, but with Broussard staring me down, I didn't dare refute Zack's statement.

"Let's table that for now and concentrate on the issue of Price's misdeeds involving women. Oliver, you need to track down Price's brother. Quinn, follow up with the AICE organizer. Maybe they know who T. Willis is. If not, visit the school library and start going through yearbooks. The fact that a sonogram of a developing fetus was found in Price's desk can't be ignored."

"One other thing," I said as everyone got to their feet. "I dropped Price's laptop off with the tech people. I keep hoping we'll find something like an email or a text from his phone that might give us a hint."

"I'll see if I can put a little pressure on to get those things cracked," Broussard said, nodding.

"What about me?" Acosta asked. "Should I stick with these guys, or have you got something else you want me to look into now that the graffiti case is closed?"

"Stick with Oliver and Quinn. The more eyes we have on this, the quicker we'll get it solved."

We all headed for the door, but I turned back to ask if Broussard had heard anything from Rafe about arrangements for his dad. He hadn't. I made a note to call Rafe later.

Zack waited in the hall, tapping a toe impatiently as Acosta and I emerged.

"I just talked to Price's brother, and I'm headed out to talk to him. Either of you have a problem with that?"

He didn't invite Paul to go with him, so for now, it looked like it was going to be me and Acosta working on everything else. "How about I follow up with the AICE director?"

"And I'll track Ed Cambridge down," Acosta offered.

"Excellent. We can meet back here after lunch." Then Oliver shook his head. "Better make that later—maybe fourish? Price's brother lives on the other side of Jacksonville. It'll take me that long just to drive up there."

Acosta nodded.

That would give me time to look in on the Connors and find out where they've been during the time in question as well as talk to the AICE person. "Sounds good to me."

"While you're over at the high school, drop in on Anderson's secretary. Find out who he was yelling at."

I held onto my temper. At least Oliver was letting me do the asking and not charging into Ty's office himself with more accusations Ty didn't need aired with no discretion at his office. Not trusting myself to answer without sniping back, I just waved an assent and turned on my heel.

CHAPTER 21

THE TALL, MIDDLE-AGED WOMAN STRODE into the conference room on four-inch heels and introduced herself with her hand extended. "Dr. Hawkins."

"Detective Quinn," I returned the formality.

"I understand you wanted to ask about our AICE program?" She gestured to a small grouping of upholstered chairs on the far side of the room.

I followed her lead and dropped into one of the chairs. "Not the program in general, although it would be nice to know more about it. Until I was assigned my most recent case, I didn't even know it existed. I have a son enrolled here and next year my daughter will be joining him."

"AICE stands for Advanced International Certificate of Education. It's for the brightest and most dedicated students who want to excel at both the high school and college level. As I'm sure you know, advanced placement courses are offered here and many of them qualify for college credits if passed with a high enough grade. But the AICE goes a step further and offers an international standard of achievement."

I nodded my grasp of that information and interrupted her to get to the point of my interview. "At the moment, I'm more interested, due to aspects of a case I'm currently working on, with the community volunteerism aspect. To be more specific, I understand there has been a group of students who regularly serve meals at St. Francis House."

Her pretty face registered regret. "That was the case, but we are temporarily on hold with that activity. As I'm sure you know, Pastor Price, who was our most willing adult volunteer has recently passed. He has not yet been replaced."

Passed seemed a tempered word for murder, but I let it go. I decided a direct approach would be more effective. "Were you aware that Price had been approaching young women in that group and carrying on sexual relationships with some of them?"

Now the expression of sad loss fled, and astonishment filled her face, followed swiftly by denial. "Surely not!"

"Unfortunately, surely yes," I countered.

She fell back into her chair, eyes wide with a mixture of horror and concern.

"I've spoken to a couple of the young women who are no longer students here but were members of AICE when they were. They have moved on to college, so I can't attest to whether any of the young women currently in the program might have been the recipient of his attentions. It is possible that one young woman, barely more than a girl," I corrected myself, picturing that youthful lifeless face. "A girl who recently committed suicide might have been abused, however. We don't know that for certain, but it's a possibility.

"I am shocked." Dr. Hawkins muttered. I was sure she was busy considering the awful ramifications if this information became public knowledge.

"I'm not here to impugn the program or make any of this known beyond this room and the Sheriff's office. But we are investigating the murder of Pastor Price and need to follow up on any illicit connections he might currently have had within that group."

She shook her head vehemently. "I am sure there are none."

"How can you be sure when you were not even aware that there were students he'd been with in the past?"

"What…" she broke off, took a huge breath, her teeth clamped so tight the muscles in her temples jumped. "What would you like for me to do?"

"I would like for you to interview the students you oversee in that group. Both the young women and the boys. Individually. Ask if any of them know of others who they think might have been involved."

She swallowed and nodded. "Certainly. How soon do you need to have this information?"

"The sooner the better," I responded opening my notebook. "I have a couple names you might start with. Amy Conners is the young woman I just mentioned, but she took her own life so we might never know if she was involved. The only other name I have who is currently still a student here is Ashley Kimball. We know that in the past Janey Cambridge was either approached or did have a relationship with Price." I didn't mention Madison Devers given our decision to keep her name out of any formal reports unless facts pointing at her father could no longer be ignored.

"It appears he was cagey. Our informant told us that he only got involved with girls who were over sixteen so there could never be any charge of statutory rape. He was quite the charmer and all the women we know of were convinced it was love and that they would become Mrs. Price in due course. When he lost interest or had another young woman in his sights, he left them feeling like they had done something wrong, and the breakup was entirely their own fault. Most of them failed to tell anyone about it due to embarrassment." I was stretching the assumptions to the status of truths, but I felt like that was the only way I'd get this woman's cooperation.

Dr. Hawkins shook her head. An expression of determination hardening her pretty features. "This information comes as a total shock. I had no idea anything of the kind was going on. No one breathed a word of it to me, or anyone else who would have been in charge. But I promise you, I will get to the bottom of it now that you have brought it to my attention." She stood. Her clamped jaw caused her temples to jump again.

"One other question," I halted her retreat to the door. "Do you know of a past student by the name of Willis? T. Willis?"

Dr. Hawkins brow puckered as she searched her memory. "I'm not sure if I do. How long ago would she have been a student here? I've only been in charge for two years."

There went an easy lead. "It would have been more than two years. I'll go check the school yearbooks."

She nodded and held the door for me.

I handed her my card. "Sooner would be better. I'm sure you understand."

She took the card without looking at it. "I hope this can stay between us."

"I hope so, as well," I replied starting through the door. "I would hate to damage an entire program that I'm sure has done a world of good for those fortunate enough to be a part of it."

Dr Hawkins followed me into the hall and put her hand out again. "I'll call you. May I see you out?"

"I still have to look through the yearbooks, and I'm sure you have things you need to get back to," I replied. I still had Ty's office to stop at as well, and I didn't need her to know about that.

We parted in the hallway. She strutted off on those impossibly high heels in one direction and I headed back the way I'd come which would take me right past Ty's office.

His outer door was open when I reached it, so I strode in. The door to his personal office was also open and it didn't appear anyone was inside. Good!

A youngish woman, perhaps in her late twenties, occupying a small desk just inside the outer door glanced up. "Dr. Anderson isn't in right now, but—"

I cut her off. "I'm here to speak to you."

"Oh?" She frowned. "What can I help you with, Ms...?"

"Detective," I corrected, wanting to get to the point. "I'm here to ask about an altercation I was told took place between Dr. Anderson and another man a week or so back."

"An altercation?" The woman's frown deepened.

"An argument. A loud argument."

"Dr. Anderson does not argue." Her frown fled and she smiled. "He's the nicest man. He's never angry and he treats everyone with respect." That was the Ty Anderson I knew, but then, the same things had been said about Pastor Price.

"What about someone else doing all the arguing. Loudly. Loudly enough so you couldn't have missed it unless you were not sitting at this desk or even in this room at the time." I assumed she had been here as that was what Zack had reported. Although, how he'd found out, he hadn't shared.

"Now that you mention it, I do recall something like that. But, as I said, Dr. Anderson did not do any of the yelling. The other man stormed in here, right past my desk without even looking at me and pushed Dr. Anderson's door open without leave. He didn't even bother to find out if Dr. Anderson had anyone with him, before barging in. I didn't hear the beginning of the discussion. Only the yelling before he stormed out as nasty as he'd come."

"But you don't know who it was?"

"He didn't have an appointment. I have no idea who he was, and Dr. Anderson would not tell me when I asked. He just said the man was upset and he'd calm down. I wasn't to worry about it. So, I put it out of my mind. Until just now." The woman stood, breathing hard like she'd just run a race.

"Did you hear anything that was said?" I pursued.

"Only that he thought Dr. Anderson should have called him and not just given his daughter his card and heap of bad advice."

"But you have no idea what kind of bad advice?"

The woman shook her head. "I'm sorry, but that's all I know, Detective. Is Dr. Anderson in trouble?"

"No. Certainly not." I prayed that was the case. "I wanted to know who had been to see him. That's all."

"I'm so sorry I can't help."

She looked genuinely sorry.

"No need to mention this to Dr. Anderson. I'm sure he's forgotten the incident and no need to bring it up again." If anyone was going to bring it up again, it would be me talking to Ty. Alone.

The woman nodded vigorously. "Of course. I won't mention it."

"I didn't get your name?" I held out another of my cards. "Should you learn who the man was, please give me a call."

"Of course. And I'm Cicely. Cicely Morse." She read the card, then tucked it under the edge of a little stamp dispenser shaped like the St. Augustine lighthouse.

I headed for the door. The last thing I wanted at this moment was to run into Ty himself. Not until I'd decided how to approach him about the shouting match. I also had to corner Amy Connors' parents, and I had a feeling they were not going to be in the same place, and it was already past noon. I had a four o'clock deadline. And some yearbooks to hunt down.

The librarian, seated behind an impossibly large wall of books she appeared to be cataloging, pointed over my shoulder when I asked where I could find school yearbooks.

I glanced back and saw the neat row of blue bindings on a shelf beside the door I'd just come in through. "Thanks," I tossed over my shoulder as I retraced my steps.

Handily organized by year, it was easy to find the most recent and work back. I skipped this year and the one previous. The third book from the end was a zip, as was the fourth. But in a book four years previous, I found her.

'Taylor Anne Willis' read the caption beneath a smiling senior with a very pretty face and long curling blond hair and dark brown eyes. A bio accompanied the image. I glanced around, saw a copier near the far wall of the main room, and hurried toward it. I wanted to get it copied and the book returned to the stacks before the librarian could tell me I wasn't allowed to make copies.

"Can I assist you with something?" The librarian was at my elbow as I straightened from reshelving the yearbook just a few minutes later.

"Did you know this girl?" I asked, showing her the copy I'd made and hoping there were no restrictions about copies.

"Why yes." The woman brightened. "Taylor was a lovely young woman. She volunteered here in the library. She tutored some of her fellow students that struggled with their subjects. But—"

"But what?" I asked when she stopped mid-sentence.

"Nothing really." The woman looked troubled. As if she might have said something she shouldn't.

"Did she happen to leave before graduating?" I asked, guessing at what might be behind the abrupt halt of praises.

The librarian's shoulders slumped. "It was quite unexpected and never explained. I heard she graduated. But from a different school. I'm not sure why. Her parents passed away when she was a freshman, but she was living with the family of one of her friends. I thought that was so she could complete her studies here. Taylor was also taking courses at St. John's River State College here in St. Augustine, but perhaps she finished those courses at the campus in Palatka or Orange Park?" The woman finished with a question mark as if she'd said all she knew and wasn't sure what she might add.

"Thank you. You've been most helpful." I nodded at the woman and headed for the door.

At least I knew the young woman's name. I could get her current address from her driver's license, presuming she had one.

But first I had to stop at the Connors' home, so I'd pursue that information later.

CHAPTER 22

THE CONNORS' HOME sported black bunting under each of the front windows, and a wreath of unlikely black flowers hung on the door. I rang the bell and waited.

After five minutes with no response, I rang again. The driveway was full of vehicles so they must be home, presumably with company come to offer sympathy.

When there was still no response, I stepped off the small porch and followed a brick path that snaked around the corner of the house. I heard the murmur of voices before I saw the small group of adults seated in all-weather rattan furniture arranged around an unlit fire-pit before they noticed me. I hailed them to announce my presence before I reached them and the gentleman I recognized as Mr. Connors lurched to his feet and approached.

"Detective." He offered his hand. "What can I do for you?"

I glanced at the now gawking group. "Is there somewhere we can speak in private? Is your wife here?"

"Of course. Come with me." He gestured to the adults still seated but silent, maybe hoping to listen in. "I'll just be a few minutes." Then, he led me toward the house. "My wife is in the kitchen."

Mrs. Connors was arranging finger food on platters in an old-fashioned farm-house style kitchen when we entered. She looked up, a question lifting her brows as she glanced from her husband to me and back.

"I'm sorry to bother you when you have company. I just have a few more questions I'd like to ask."

Mrs. Connors looked around her, then at her husband as if the idea of more questions filled her with confusion. He just gestured toward the front room and began walking, obviously expecting us to follow along.

Once seated in their shabby but comfortable living room, both parents leaning forward with their elbows on their knees, I sighed and dove in. "Your younger daughter, I believe her name is Lisa?"

Both parents nodded.

"Lisa thought her sister . . .," I paused. There really was no kind way to say what I had to say. "Lisa thought Amy took her life because she was despondent over a broken relationship. Do either of you know who she was dating?"

Mr. Connors harrumphed. "Amy never told me anything after her first date with Gary."

"That's because you were rude to Gary," Mrs. Connors shot at him. "Gary was a nice boy, and he didn't deserve it." She glanced back at me. "My husband is the kind of father they make jokes about … waiting for their daughter to come home armed with a shotgun."

Mr. Connors harrumphed again. "He wasn't good enough for her."

"He was a nice boy."

My antennae shot up. "Had Amy dated him recently? Is that the relationship she was upset about?" A father with a shotgun might just have handguns in his arsenal as well. And the know-how to use them along with a rudimentary understanding of explosives.

"Oh, no. That was more than a year ago," Amy's mother said sadly. "She didn't date for a while after she and Gary broke up. Lately, I had a feeling she might be seeing someone, but she didn't confide in me. She never went out on Friday or Saturday nights like most teens do. I'm not sure when she would have had time for a relationship, truthfully. She was into the AICE program at school and spent most of her time studying or working on the homeless meal project."

Well, that answered one of my questions. "But you have no idea who she might have been in a relationship with."

Mrs. Connors shook her head. "Relationship might not be the right word for it. I think she maybe had a crush on some boy she either studied with or worked with in AICE." A tear leaked down the woman's face. "I wish she had shared more with me. And now it's too late." The tears fell in earnest now and Mr. Connors was glaring at me for being the cause.

I got to my feet and thanked them for their time. "I'm sorry to have bothered you."

"Was there something specific you needed to know?" Mr. Connors said to my back as he followed me to the door. "A good reason for you to come barging in here and bringing up difficult subjects?"

If he'd had a shotgun handy, I wasn't entirely sure he wouldn't have used it on me.

"I'm sorry for your loss," I said as I reached the door and turned with one last question before letting myself out. "Where were you and your wife the day your church was destroyed?" Easier to get an honest answer about the church than Price's murder.

"We were in Gainesville. Making arrangements for our daughter's funeral."

"You didn't plan to have services for her at Church of Peace?"

"Amy was dedicated to Jesus at the church my wife grew up in out in Gainesville. Just seemed right."

"And you were there all day?"

"A few days. My wife found comfort with her family around her. We went out right after—" He swallowed hard. "After Amy left us. We returned yesterday. That was the first we knew of Pastor Price's demise or the destruction of our church. A very sad homecoming, I'm afraid."

If he only knew. Mrs. Connors remained on the couch weeping. Mr. Connors clearly wanted me gone.

So, I got gone.

Acosta held up the pot he had been pouring himself a cup of coffee from, offering to pour one for me. I nodded and settled into one of the chairs to compare notes while we waited for Zack and Broussard to show up.

"How did you make out?" I asked the young detective as he delivered my coffee and joined me at the table.

"Cambridge is in the clear. He was at the station all day until they got the call-out for the church explosion. Guess he was just blowing off steam and probably gloating a little at the karma of it all."

Zack and Broussard hurried in together at this juncture so, Acosta repeated his day for them.

"How about Price's brother?" I was eager to know if we had an additional lead to follow up on.

Zack shook his head. "Another dead end, I'm afraid. Wesley Price was out of the country. He just got back yesterday to be greeted with the news of his brother's passing."

"If what I've heard is true, there might not have been much in the way of grieving."

Zack snorted. "Hardly. More like glee if that's the right word. He announced right off that his brother got what he deserved. If anything, he was disgruntled that as the only remaining family member, now he's got to get down here and waste time wrapping up his brother's affairs while he should be getting back to work. Hah! Business affairs, that is."

"And you, Quinn?" Broussard turned to me.

"I started with Dr. Hawkins. She was completely blind-sided by my assertion of affairs between Winston Price and some of the young women in the AICE program. But she pulled herself together and quickly agreed to talk to a few people and get back to me if she learned anything that might help us determine who did the sleazebag in."

Broussard raised an eyebrow at my denigration of our victim but didn't bother to correct me. "How about the Connors?"

"Another dead-end. They were in Gainesville. I haven't had time to check the alibi, but I doubt he had a reason to lie. They were staying with Mrs. Connors' parents and making funeral arrangements at the church where Mrs. Connors grew up and where the couple were married. Apparently, Amy, the dead girl, was dedicated at that church as well."

"I told you," Zack jumped in. Ty Anderson is looking better and better for this."

"It's a set-up, Zack."

"How is it a set-up when his wife brings explosives to Central? Or that the 'Slease-bag' as you called him, picketed the Andersons' son's funeral? Or that he has a temper?"

"Ty Anderson is the last man to let anger get the better of him," I countered.

"He was heard yelling at a man who came into his office at the school. That sounds like uncontrolled temper to me."

"I'm not sure where you got your information, Zack, but I decided to check that accusation out while I was at the school today. And it was not Ty who was doing the yelling."

"Then who was it?"

Paul Acosta and Broussard watched the two of us go at it like they were at a tennis match.

"It was whoever barged into his office, ignored his secretary and even the possibility that Ty might have had a student with him in his office at the time. Unfortunately, the secretary has no idea who the man was. She'd never seen him before, and he didn't have an appointment. He left without even speaking to her. That's who was doing all the yelling. His secretary, Cicely Morse, insisted that Dr. Anderson never raised his voice. Not then or ever."

"Still—"

"Think about it, Zack. You get an anonymous call that the murder weapon is hidden in Ty's truck. How exactly did this caller know there was supposed to be a gun under Ty's front seat unless he put it there himself. And then he got the wrong truck.

"Ty and Seth both drive Dodge Rams. Same year, same color. And both men are involved in the Habitat for Humanity project which, currently is the house out on CR 206 where Seth was accosted two nights ago. If your caller was the same person who was making a scene in Ty's office, and possibly the same person who killed Price, maybe he also felt justified in trying to frame Dr. Anderson for whatever perceived wrong he thinks Anderson is guilty of. What a golden opportunity it must have seemed to find what he thought was Anderson's truck untended on that site. Only Seth came out and surprised him. Unfortunately, Seth got knocked over the head before he realized anyone was messing with his truck."

I sat back, satisfied that I'd thrust a spoke in Zack's wheel.

"Hate to say it, but Jesse's scenario fits," Broussard observed. "Now we just need to figure out who that person of interest is. What about video? Any cameras that might have caught the action at the school?"

I shook my head. "Not in the counselor's office. Something about privacy. There are cameras on the main entrance and two others used by students, but none in or even around his office. I checked what footage they had but didn't see anything. It's not likely whoever it was worked there, or Miss Morse would have known him. I have to assume he left by a door without cameras."

"Damn!" Broussard dropped his tablet on the table in frustration.

"But I did get more info on the student who sent that sonogram to Price. Her name is Taylor Willis. Dr. Hawkins is new and never met or heard about Willis, but the librarian was more forthcoming.

CHAPTER 23

BROUSSARD SUGGESTED WE ALL FINISH UP the paperwork for today's efforts and go home, get some rest, and maybe come back tomorrow with fresh eyes and a new perspective.

"If you can get me a list of girls the jerk supposedly abused, I can dig around and see if any of their fathers or brothers attended UF," Paul offered.

"It's more like innocents he seduced," I corrected as I pulled a sheet of paper from my notebook and scribbled all the names I knew, leaving out Madison. I already knew Deputy Devers was not a UF grad. I handed it to Paul. "Thanks. See you both in the morning."

One last task before heading home.

I returned to my desk where I tapped into the data base of Florida driver's licenses, praying Taylor Willis had not married in the three years since leaving St. Augustine. But the first name was unique enough I might find her even if she had.

Remarkably, there were three licensed drivers by the name of Taylor Willis. One had graduated ten years earlier and lived in Miami. Ruled her out. The second had held her license for a mere four months and lived in Tallahassee. The third had to be our girl. Her birth date fit the age range. She was living in a small town called Starke between here and Gainesville. Better yet, the image on her license matched the one I'd copied from the yearbook.

I copied the new information into my notebook and reached for the phone. I had plenty of time to drive out to Starke before knocking off for the day.

Taylor Willis was nothing like I'd expected. She greeted me at the door wearing a flour-dusted apron with a small child hiding behind it.

"Please. Come on in," she invited glancing at her hands before wiping them on the apron which did little to remove the remnants of whatever she was busy with in the kitchen, before offering one to me. Then she hoisted the child onto one hip and backed into the hall to allow me access.

"I've got cookies in the oven, so I hope you won't mind talking in the kitchen."

"Lead the way," I responded, my nose already twitching at the scent of fresh baked chocolate chip cookies.

We no sooner entered the kitchen than a bell dinged. Ms. Willis reached for a potholder, gestured to a comfortable looking rocker in one corner, and opened the oven. I held my questions until she'd transferred the cookies to a cooling rack and sat down.

"What about the AICE program did you want to know?" She asked, as she lifted the child onto her lap. "Excuse me. I should have introduced you. This is my daughter Sophia. Sophia, this is Detective Quinn."

The child stared at me with solemn pale blue eyes. Eyes she'd clearly gotten from her father given Taylor's dark brown ones. "Hello, Sophia," I said, not sure if I should offer to shake hands with a toddler.

Sophia glanced at her mother, then back at me. "Hewow." Then she covered her face with both hands.

"She's shy," Taylor apologized, then her face went serious. "AICE is a long way in my rear-view mirror. I'm not sure what I can add to anything you already know about it.

I took a deep breath and got to the point. "Actually, I wanted to discuss one of the AICE volunteers. A Pastor Winston Price."

Shock replaced puzzlement and Taylor appeared to grow paler. "Did he send you here?"

I shook my head. "Why would you think that?"

Taylor wrapped her arms about her daughter and pulled her more firmly against her chest. "I don't want him in Sophia's life."

I wondered if this subject had come up recently, and if someone in Taylor's life had suggested approaching the Pastor. I put the query into words.

Taylor jerked her head side to side.

"Why would you not wish your daughter to know who her father was eventually?"

"He didn't want her when he had the chance. And I put that all behind me. I came out to live with my aunt. I got my degree all on my own, thank you, and I am more than capable of taking care of Sophia without him now."

"So, you live here with your aunt? How about an uncle?"

"Aunt Gloria was never married."

"A boyfriend?"

Taylor frowned. "Me or Aunt Gloria? Actually, it doesn't matter. Neither of us have a boyfriend. Aunt Gloria never leaned that way to start with and I've been too busy with school and Sophia. But why does it matter?"

I'd already learned Taylor was an only child and her parents deceased. So, unless her aunt or she were up to the task, I was pretty sure I could cross them off my list of persons of interest. I decided to watch her reaction to the news of Price's death before asking where they were the night he was murdered.

"You won't have to worry about Winston Price wanting to be a part of your daughter's life," I began, and watched her shoulders relax. "He was murdered."

Now it was Taylor's turn to fix me with wide eyes. Clearly shock was her main reaction. I was pretty sure I didn't have to ask where she was on the night in question, but I asked anyway.

"I...I—" Clearly still too shocked to comprehend. "I was here. I mean, I was—What night?"

I repeated the date.

It was almost as if she was counting backward on her fingers as she considered my question. "I was here," she finally repeated. "It was

Aunt Gloria's bridge night. And I filled in for one of the regular ladies. You don't think I had anything to do with Winston's death, do you?" She was finally coming to terms with the reason for my visit, but even less alarmed than before. Either she was the best actress I'd ever met, or she and her aunt were totally out of the running for our perp.

I got to my feet. "I'm sorry to have been the bearer of bad news. Although, I guess it's not all that disturbing considering you put that part of your life behind you and have created a new one."

"I'll be honest. When you asked to come out to talk to me about AICE, I was afraid. I've always been a little afraid that Winston would change his mind and show up on my doorstep one day. It's a relief to know that will never happen."

Taylor showed me to the door. Sophia, now nodding off, had her head tucked into her mother's neck and her thumb thrust firmly into her mouth.

"Thank you," Taylor said as I turned to go. "For coming all the way out here to tell me, I mean."

"I'm glad it's brought you some measure of closure," I told her, meaning it more than I usually did when I offered words of solace.

She was still standing in her doorway as I pulled out, illuminated by the light from the hall behind her.

Another dead end.

CHAPTER 24

WHEN I PULLED INTO MY DRIVEWAY Ty's truck was parked between my drive and his own. I figured he must have had a houseful of company earlier and just hadn't had a moment to move it as I eased around it and into my usual spot.

I trudged up the stairs expecting a dismally quiet house and was pleasantly surprised when I heard music from Mike's room where he was practicing on his guitar. Murphy danced around my feet with happy little yips making me welcome.

"Hey, Murph." I bent to scratch the golden fur behind her ears. Several knots of fur proclaimed my having ignored her grooming for far too long. It would be cathartic to go sit out on the deck and brush her.

I secured my weapon, slipped into shorts and a T-shirt, then stopped long enough to grab a beer from the fridge and her brush. I called the dog and headed for my retreat.

Murphy enjoyed the brushing, but she hated the untangling of knots part. She protested more than once, but she was getting better at letting me do what needed doing. Or maybe she was just glad to see me and being more patient than usual lest I leave again.

"You always sneak into your house and fail to say hi?"

I jerked around, surprised by the sound of Seth's voice as much as his presence in my home. "Sorry. Didn't know you were here. Mike was busy and I didn't want to interrupt," I excused my lapse of manners and shook my head at my previous assumptions. That tipster with the gun wasn't the only one who had mistaken Seth's truck for Ty's.

Seth lowered himself into the chaise next to the one I was perched on while brushing the dog.

"Feeling better?" I asked.

"Much," he replied. I figured it was time I brought your family home and got back to taking care of myself." He reached for the brush and took over for me.

Murphy, traitor to the core, leaned back against his knees and tipped her head up, offering no resistance at all to the grooming.

"Any closer to finding out who murdered Price and blew up his church?" Seth's hands moved rhythmically while Murphy lapped up the attention. Clearly, she had enjoyed her stay at his place and now considered him part of her pack.

"I don't suppose you know who barged into Ty Anderson's office last week?"

His face registered complete surprise. "Didn't know anyone had. Is it related to your investigation? I thought Ty was cleared when your partner found the murder weapon in my car instead of his."

"My temporary partner," I clarified.

"What about the kid you and Rafe were working with on the graffiti case. I presume that must be connected considering whose church it was."

"Our sergeant has him working with me and Zack now, but the graffiti turns out to be a moot point."

"Moot?"

"Yeah. Acosta – that's the kid, only he's not really a kid, finally caught up with him. A guy who calls himself Dusty and lives out of his truck. He's a vet and had a beef with Pastor Price over a lot of things, including the picketing of funerals, and apparently the seducing of young women. He freely admitted to the artwork. But he's not our guy." It suddenly occurred to me that we never asked Dusty how he knew about the debauchery. Another loose end to check out tomorrow.

"I guess that would have been too easy." Seth finished with Murphy and set the brush down. "I'd stay and visit, but I'm told I need to rest. It's past time to head home and put my feet up. Besides, you look pretty beat yourself."

He got to his feet and Murphy danced ahead of him into the house while I followed, disappointed that he was leaving now that I'd just come home.

As Seth reached the door, he turned, gently cupped my chin in his palm and lowered his head to mine. The kiss was gentle. Completely undemanding and yet filled with what felt like longing. Maybe all the longing was on my part, but I wanted to believe it was on his as well.

"When you're not all wrapped up in this case, let's do dinner. You can pick the place."

"I'd like that."

He was right, of course. I needed to focus on the case. And when I was with him, I needed to be wholly with him, not constantly mulling over some bit of information or conjecture about who shot Price.

One last light kiss and he was gone, his footsteps retreating down the stairs. A few moments later, the sound of the Ram's engine turning over and then the crunch of big tires on gravel.

I leaned my back against the door. Murphy sat looking at me hopefully. She probably needed to go out. I hunted down a leash, and we headed for the stairs.

I followed her around the yard, across the drive to the rough uncut grass on the far side, back to the mowed lawn and then back to the rough.

"Could you just find a place and go?" I asked the dog, a little frustrated. I'd already managed to blow more than an hour and I still had to haul out my laptop and get to work.

"Mrs. Quinn?"

I glanced over my shoulder and saw Kiara hurrying across from her parents' yard.

"I just saw this and, well, I don't know if it's connected but I thought it might be, so here." She thrust a clipping from a newspaper in my direction.

I glanced at it. An obituary. For a minute, I thought it was Amy Connors. The picture looked eerily like the pale still body Rafe and I had found in her. Then I looked closer. Under the image of a girl about the same age as Amy, same pale blond hair, and blue eyes, it read: Elizabeth Merrick. I did the math. She'd only been seventeen when she died. I speed-read the rest of the short text. No cause of death mentioned.

"Did you know her?" I asked Kiara, who had waited while I read.

"Not really. But my sister does. Did. Keisha says word is that Lizzy died because of a reaction to a drug she took. Keisha says if you ask around, you can get some kind of pills that are supposed to cure ulcers but do a pretty good at ending pregnancies so who knows how many kids in trouble have tried it?"

All this was said in a hushed rush. Like I needed to know it all yesterday, but she didn't want to be overheard. Except there wasn't anyone to hear her except me and Murphy who had finally done her business and returned to claim a belly rub from Kiara.

Kiara gave in to the dog's obvious desire and squatted to rub said belly.

Another lead to follow up on tomorrow. Good. I needed to keep Zack looking in any direction other than Ty.

"Well, I've got to get going. I'm headed back to New York tomorrow. Just wanted to pass on this bit before I left."

"Thanks for your help." I opened my arms and pulled the young woman into a hug. "Safe flight. I'll look forward to seeing you at Christmas."

"Me, too," she sing-songed as she waved and headed back to her parents' house.

I trudged back up my stairs considering the best plan of attack for the morning. Perhaps Zack and I should go together this time and send Paul off to hunt down Dusty again to ask how he knew about the Pastor's sexual exploits. Two of the images Paul had shown us clearly referenced sex in one way or another but we hadn't thought to ask if he knew any of the young women in the AICE. It was likely he'd been in line for a free meal at St. Francis House a few times and overheard rumors of the Pastor's activities there. In any case, Paul could handle that interview.

To my shame, I'd not taken my commander's request to play nice with Zack very seriously. It was time I grew up and focused on results rather than insults.

Zack thumbed through a Highlights for Children magazine while I studied the wall of children's photos lining Dr. Merrick's office walls. The kids ranged from four to fourteen or so, all with gleaming teeth and broad smiles. No telling if they were his patients or professional models mounted there to encourage his young patients to brush regularly.

"Detectives?" The strangely high-pitched male voice spoke from a doorway with a hall beyond, presumably leading to his dental treatment rooms. My initial reaction was deflation. This man just did not look like a killer.

Dressed in scrubs decorated with blue Smurfs, the man couldn't have stood more than five foot eight and probably weighed less than a hundred pounds soaking wet. And then there was the voice.

Zack glanced at me and shrugged. Clearly, he was just as unimpressed with the likelihood we were looking at a killer as I was.

"Please, come into my office," Dr. Merrick said, sweeping a hand in an ushering gesture. He then turned and walked ahead. Even his gait suggested anything but a man capable of blowing up a church or killing its pastor.

His office was equally unimpressive. He did have the requisite diplomas framed on a wall beside his desk, one from Harvard and another from the University of North Carolina. Not a Gator man. In contrast, the opposite wall featured several of the Looney Tunes characters. Bugs Bunny with just two prominent incisors, the Tasmanian Devil with a menacing array of sharply pointed teeth and Daffy Duck with no teeth at all.

"How may I help you?" the doctor said as he lowered himself to the chair behind the desk. "My receptionist said it was about an investigation?" He ended on an upbeat, making that part of his welcome a question as well.

Zack remained standing. He liked looking down at anyone he was questioning. I was sure he enjoyed the intimidation factor, but in this case, he'd still be looking down even if he sat. I seated myself, hoping he'd take the hint. He did. Then made a show of pulling his mini-iPad from his pocket and waking it up.

"We are investigating the events at the Church of Peace earlier this week," I said before Zack could start.

Dr. Merrick didn't even blink. If he was our guy, he was a very cool customer. "I heard about that. But it's not my church so I didn't think much about it. Sad, though. It was a pretty building."

"Your daughter didn't have anything to do with the church or any of its congregation?" Zack asked, a little aggressively, considering the man's daughter was dead.

"I'm sorry for your loss," I jumped in to soften Zack's question.

Merrick looked away toward the window and it was clear his eyes had filled with tears even though none escaped to dampen his cheeks. He finally turned back to us, somewhat composed again. "Thank you. But, like I said, Peace is not our church. I know – knew all Lizzy's friends and I don't think any of them worship there either."

"What about her friends at AICE?"

"AICE? What has that to do with Church of Peace?"

"It's our understanding that Pastor Price was a volunteer serving meals to the homeless at St Francis House."

Merrick looked confused. This couldn't be our guy.

"And members of AICE volunteered for that program as well. We just wondered if your daughter had been involved?" Zack pressed.

"I think she was, once or twice. But she was more focused on her studies. She had early acceptance to Harvard. Did you know? And she'll never go now." His eyes glazed over again, but he pulled himself together more quickly this time and glanced at his watch. "Is there anything else you needed to ask? I have my next appointment in just a few minutes. In fact, she might already be waiting for me."

Zack and I stood. If we needed more, we knew where he worked, and it seemed unlikely he'd skip town.

"We're sorry for intruding and sorry for your loss," I repeated as we headed to the door.

Merrick didn't say anything else as we let ourselves out and headed for the waiting room.

"He's not our guy," Zack said as we climbed into his unmarked car. "We're back to Ty Anderson. Unless Acosta turns up a new lead or two.

I had expected him to reiterate his belief that Ty was still a person of interest, but remembering the promise I made to myself earlier, I remained silent.

"You are focused on the wrong guy," I insisted once we were back at Central and waiting for Acosta to show up.

Zack leaned back, balanced one casual foot on his other knee and smirked. "I'm focused where all the evidence is aimed."

"Except for one thing," I replied, dropping into the chair opposite his desk.

He cocked an eyebrow at me. "And that would be….?"

"Let me ask you a question. Do you believe that blowing up the Church of Peace was intended for total destruction?"

"That's usually the purpose for blowing things up."

"And the obliteration of the good pastor's body?" I added. "Or at least destroying any evidence of how he actually died?"

Zack shrugged. "It's possible, but where is this going? And what difference does it make?"

"I talked to one of the guys from the bomb squad. I wanted to know how there had been remarkably less damage than one might assume for such an event. And you know what he told me?" I hurried on before Zack could interrupt. "The bomb tech said whoever set the bomb hadn't taken into consideration all that glass. It shattered too easily allowing the force of a blast that might have brought an entire brick building down to release most of its energy straight out through the wall of glass. The expert's assessment was that whoever set that bomb was not skilled and was just copying things he'd seen on TV shows on YouTube.

"And that," I paused for effect, "Leaves Ty out."

Zack frowned but persisted. "And how do you figure that exonerates Anderson?"

"One of your bits 'of evidence'," I emphasized the word evidence, "is that Ty had the knowledge to assemble and explode a bomb. And that explosives were found in his home by his wife and turned in to the Sheriff's office. But don't you think that an ex-Navy SEAL with plenty of experience in explosives would have known about the effect an entire wall of glass would have? And perhaps done the job a little differently?"

Zack's frown deepened and he dropped his foot to the floor. "Maybe he didn't intend to destroy the church or mask the murder. Maybe he just wanted to make an example of the Pastor?"

"Most people don't resort to killing to make an example of someone. I think whoever killed Pastor Price had a far stronger motive than making an example of people who picket soldier funerals. Like maybe avenging a young woman preyed on by the pastor."

"Like who?" Zach challenged. "We just talked to one of your hunches and ruled him out. Price's brother was old news and out of the country. Cambridge was at a conference. And you reported that the Connors were in Gainesville. And the girl who had Price's kid is happily settled in Starke. Who's left?"

"Like whoever stormed into Ty's office blaming Ty for giving his daughter bad advice. We know Lizzie Merrick was not the only young woman who got involved with Price, so there could be other fathers with a beef against Price.

"We've talked to two fathers whose daughters were involved with the man, but ruled them out, so they likely weren't the angry visitor to Anderson's office. Who do you suggest we look at next?"

"I tried getting that information out of Ty, but he insists it's a matter of confidentiality."

"Even to save his own ass?" Zack's eyebrows rose.

"Even to save his own ass," I agreed. "Something one of the girls I talked to said something that gave me another thought, though. She said she heard of a girl who got pregnant, not one of Price's conquests, but just a kid who got knocked up by her teenage boyfriend. The boy wanted her to get an abortion, and she went to Ty for advice. And Ty told her to talk to her parents who loved her and would be her best source of support.

"Only that girl didn't follow Ty's advice. She went to some doctor some friend of hers knew about who gave her some of those pills they make for ulcers that are also effective for ending a pregnancy," I repeated Kiara's information. Kiara had given me the obit for Lizzie Merrick, but given our interview with Dr. Merrick, I ruled him out, but kept thinking that it might apply to some other girl.

"How does that help us now?"

"What if whoever is responsible has a daughter, and the girl went to Ty after Price got her pregnant and dumped her. Ty would have suggested telling her parents. But suppose the girl got some pills from this doctor first and then told her parents that Ty suggested that course of action after it was all over, and it was too late for her parents to object."

"Anderson isn't responsible for either the pregnancy or the abortion, so I don't get the father's beef with the counselor?" Zach looked a little less skeptical.

"Even though Ty would never advise any girl to get an abortion, I'm guessing that maybe a father might believe the daughter and thought he had. If this alleged father did kill Pastor Price, maybe he thought he could kill two birds with one stone and get back at Ty by planting the gun in his truck to get him blamed. Except he got the wrong truck."

"In that case, it's time to interview all the fathers involved. We've only ruled out three." Zach stood. Where is Acosta? Have you heard from Dr. Hawkins?"

CHAPTER 25

PAUL ACOSTA KNOCKED on the doorframe, then entered the office without waiting for an invite. "Dusty said he had help with the penis graffiti and that's who told him about Price and the girls from the high school."

"Did he have any names?" Zack fired back.

"Sorta. At least a first name. He never asked for the man's last name. Judy is the guy's daughter and the man who helped paint the church was Joe."

"How does Dusty know the guy?" I asked.

"Now that's the curious part. Dusty says he went to an AA meeting. He never mentioned being an alcoholic when we talked the first time. Recovering alcoholic. He had a bad week and went to a meeting. One of the guys there talked about his daughter and admitted that he'd gone off the wagon after he found out his precious little girl had been defiled by a man old enough to be her father.

"Anyway, when it was Dusty's turn to share, he confessed to having been the artist who'd been doing the graffiti at the Church of Peace. When the meeting broke up, this guy Joe caught up with him in the parking lot and asked when he planned his next art project at Church of Peace. Next thing Dusty knows, Joe is begging to go with him to help paint, and Dusty says sure. That was when the most lurid of the sex stuff got done and most of the ideas for that graffiti were Joe's. Dusty was impressed with Joe's talent, too. The guy came back to help again on the soldier thing right before the church got blown up."

"Did this Joe guy happen to mention who defiled his little girl? Or have a last name?" Zack asked, sinking back into his chair.

"We don't share names at meetings. And he didn't say who the dirty old guy was at the meeting, but he admitted it when they planned their subject matter for the graffiti. Judy, that's the daughter, was another of the pastor's conquests."

"Let's go see your Dr. Hawkins." Zack was back on his feet.

"She said she'd call when she had any information," I objected, thinking Dr. Hawkins wasn't the sort to be pushed. She'd call when she thought she had helpful information.

"But she surely knows who Judy is and where she lives," Zack said as he headed for the door. "You coming or not?"

No way was Zack leaving me out. I hurried after him, thanking Paul for his help as I pushed past him.

"What should I do?" Paul asked.

"Add this information to the file."

"But—"

I ignored this last plea since Zack was halfway to the exit and I didn't have time for a longer discussion.

"The only Judy we've had in the program graduated two years ago," Dr. Hawkins told us after we'd waited more than a half hour for her return from a scheduled class.

"But there was a Judy in the program. What was her last name? Do you have an address for her parents?" Zack asked.

"I'm not sure . . ." Hawkins hesitated.

"We think she may have been one of Pastor Price's conquests," I suggested in a more supplicating tone. "And we have reason to believe her father may have been involved in the graffiti painted on the Church of Peace leading up to the explosion and the death of the pastor."

"I see," she drawled, as if buying time to come up with an excuse for not sharing the information.

Considering that lists of AICE participants, present and past, would be on file in the school office, I doubted we needed to get a warrant. I got to my feet and glanced at Zack, who glowered at the woman. "We can get that information in the school office."

Dr. Hawkins bit her lip, then stood and walked to a file cabinet in the corner of her office. After just a few minutes, she pulled a slender green folder from the drawer and returned to her desk. She slid a piece of stationery from a flowered box on the corner of her desk and began writing. Then she stood and handed me the paper with the girl's full name, parents' names, and an address in the more affluent part of town. Underneath were three more names: Amy Conners, Elizabeth Merrick, and Shelley Cambridge.

"And these girls?" I asked pointing to the additions.

"These are the only students who any of their classmates thought might have had a relationship with Winston Price in the past two or three years. Amy Connors tragically took her own life recently. Miss Merrick passed away some months back. Such a shame. So much talent. So much promise." Dr. Hawkins shook her head sadly. "Shelley is still in the program, but Judy graduated, and they've lost touch with her."

"Thank you for your cooperation," I said as I turned to go.

"Will you keep me apprised?" Hawkins followed me to the door.

"I will call if anything new develops," I promised vaguely as I headed for the door with Zack pushing past me.

Zack drove like we were on the way to a fire. I pried my hand off the armrest and my eyes off the traffic he was weaving in and out of to consult my notes. "Cambridge is the fireman. We already know he's not a person of interest. And the Connors aren't likely either. We talked to Dr. Merrick yesterday."

Zack briefly glanced my way with a scowl, then back to the road, finally slowing as we entered the expensive Ponte Vedra area.

The Kimball's home was an impressive Spanish style mansion perched on a dune overlooking the Atlantic Ocean, and not far from the Players Golf Course. The long winding drive ended in a fork, one side continuing around a circle past the front door, the other branching off to end in front of a garage that would accommodate at least four vehicles. At the moment, there was only one vehicle visible. A navy blue, late-model BMW.

We parked in the holly-bordered circular driveway at the foot of a broad set of steps that led to the front door. The doorbell was answered by a maid wearing a frilly black uniform I would have thought outdated years ago. We asked if Mr. Kimball was at home. He was, and we were ushered to a small room of indeterminant use just off a vast main foyer so lofty it echoed.

A few minutes later, a tall, distinguished looking man in his mid-fifties strode in. "Good afternoon, detectives. How may I assist you?"

"May we sit? Is this a good place to talk? We have a few questions for you," Zack asked in an unusually conciliating tone. Apparently, there were people whom Zack held in some sense of esteem.

"We can talk here," Kimball answered reaching behind himself to ease the door closed.

We all sat, Zack on one of two matching chairs, Mr. Kimball on the other. I perched on the end of a couch long enough to seat at least six comfortably, but close enough to Zack that we both faced our host.

"I believe you know a man who goes by the name of Dusty," I began.

Kimball was a cool customer. No reaction to the name at all.

"And I believe after making his acquaintance at a recent meeting, you volunteered to assist him in decorating the Church of Peace with some pretty lurid graffiti."

Still no reaction.

"You have a daughter named Judy?" Zack prodded gently.

Kimball brightened. "Why yes, I do. She's at Stanford studying Political Science. She plans to go on to law school after that." He was clearly proud of his little girl. No wonder he went off the deep end when he found out about Price. But that would have been over a year ago. Why wait until now to retaliate?

"So, about the graffiti?" I was eager to get back to the topic. Judy might become a lawyer one day, but she wasn't going to do her father any good if he ended up needing one now.

"Do I need a lawyer?"

"About the graffiti? Probably not. The complainant was not pressing charges and has since passed away. No one else appears eager to pursue the issue. Were you involved with a homeless man called Dusty and the defilement of the church or not?"

Kimball remained silent for a long time. Zack also remained unusually silent, awaiting his reply.

"Mr. Kimball?" I pushed.

His shoulders slumped. "Regrettable action on my part. I was angry and it seemed like just punishment."

"When did you find out Pastor Price had seduced Judy?" Seemed like Zack was willing for me to do all the questioning now.

"About two months ago. I overheard Judy talking about the man with a friend of hers when she was home from college over the summer break. She doesn't know I know, and I would like to keep it that way. My wife doesn't know anything, and I don't want her to find out. It would break her heart."

"It would break her heart that Judy was taken in by Price, or that you had a hand in defiling his church?"

"Both, I guess. I'm ashamed of my involvement now, but it was cathartic," Kimball admitted with a rueful tip of his head. "I knew it was wrong after the first time, but I was still hurting when Dusty asked if I wanted to get back at Price and his minions for picketing soldier funerals. My brother died fighting for our country. How could I say no?"

That explained Miss Wilson having seen two tall men the day the final artwork was added to the church windows. But that was several days before the Pastor's death and the explosion at the church.

"Where were you on the night of twenty-fifth?"

His eyes widened at that question. "The night the church blew up?"

"Yes, that night. Where were you and can anyone confirm it?"

"It's just a formality," Zack interjected.

"I was at a business conference in Annapolis, Maryland. I heard about the explosion and the pastor's death on my return. Justice, if you ask me, but I had nothing to do with it. Anyone at my place of business can verify that." He reached into his pocket and pulled out an elegant silver card case from which he extracted a business card. He held it out to Zack.

Zack pocketed the card without looking at it and got to his feet. "Thank you, Mr. Kimball. We appreciate you taking the time to speak to us."

Kimball and I stood as well. "And there won't be any repercussions about my unfortunate choice of retribution?"

Zack shook his head without making any verbal promises that he might not be able to keep.

Kimball showed us to the door and stood watching as we returned to our vehicle.

"Another dead end." It was the most defeated tone I'd ever heard from Zack.

CHAPTER 26

WHETHER I'D MANAGED TO CONVINCE Zack to look somewhere besides Ty or not would remain to be seen. But for now, right this minute, I was going to just erase the last troubled days from my head and enjoy a nice glass of wine. Or maybe even a tumbler with some well-aged Scotch.

Murphy greeted me at the door with all her usual enthusiasm, then went to sniff her leash. Was this a hint that I'd been ignoring her of late?

"You need to go out, girl?" I asked the dog.

She wagged eagerly, started for the door, doubled back, and wagged again.

"Well, Mom's got to change. Can you wait just a minute?"

Good grief! I was carrying on a conversation with a dog. Murphy didn't seem distressed by the detour to my room to lock up my sidearm and change into a pair of shorts and flipflops. A few minutes later we were on our way to the beach.

The cool evening air was pleasant and calming, as was the rote of the sea. The glorious pink and mauve tinged with gold and yellow promised a glorious sunset if I'd been facing west on the waterway instead of east on the Atlantic Ocean. It was a beautiful night and I planned to put the whole Price mystery out of my head and enjoy it.

Murphy bounded toward the water, but I called her back. It took her half a day to dry off and the last time I let her swim at night, she hopped onto my bed, and I ended up having to change my sheets and quilt.

I found a random piece of driftwood and threw it as far as I could, and my puppy happily chased it down and brought it back to drop at my feet. I tossed it again, enjoying these moments of unstressed time. But dark was creeping in and, having not brought a flashlight, we finally had to head home.

Mike was standing in the middle of the living room with the remote in his hand when Murphy and I topped the stairs and stepped in.

"Hey, Mom." He turned to acknowledge my arrival. "Anything you particularly want to watch tonight?"

I shrugged. "Anything's good. But what about supper? You eaten?"

"I got a pizza. I left you some. How about Field of Dreams? You ever seen it before? It's an old movie, but it looks good." Mike called after me as I headed for the kitchen and the promised pizza.

"Key it up. I'll be right in." I whirled one finger in the air.

I had seen the movie before, but it had been long enough ago that I wasn't sure how it even ended. A good choice considering it wasn't a mystery or thriller which was Mike's usual choice. I settled into the recliner, pushed it back and prepared to enjoy a good old-fashioned night at home with my boy.

"Hey, Mom?"

Someone was shaking my shoulder. It felt like I was crawling out of a well, as I pried my eyes open to see Mike bending over me. Alarm suddenly hit, and I sat up fast.

"What's wrong?"

"Nothing. I just thought you might be more comfortable in bed. Your head was kind of hanging to the side."

Now that he mentioned it, my neck did feel a little stiff. I glanced at my watch. Even the late night news was over, and Mike had turned off the TV.

"I'm sorry," I apologized getting to my feet. "I wasn't very good company tonight, was I? Hope you enjoyed the movie." And I still didn't know how Field of Dreams ended.

"It was okay," he said noncommittally. "I walked Murphy, too. See ya in the morning." He stopped to blow me a kiss as he headed down the hall to his room.

I wasted no time following him. Maybe a good night's sleep and I'd be refreshed and have a whole new perspective on my investigation come morning.

Halfway to Central, my mind turning over the possible people to interview or reinterview, my phone buzzed. I clicked the answer button on my steering wheel without checking the screen to see who might be calling.

"Detective Quinn?" a familiar voice asked.

"Mrs. Harker?" I replied, wondering what new information she might have.

"Madison was here for dinner last night and we got talking about Pastor Price and wondering if you were close to figuring out who did it. I know, I know," she rushed on. "You can't tell me, but we were still wondering, and something came up that I wasn't sure you knew about, so I thought I'd call just in case."

Anything new would be helpful, but I didn't want to sound too desperate. "Any new information is always welcome, Mrs. Harker. As I'm sure I've told you before." I turned on my blinker and pulled over so I could take notes if necessary.

"Madison was telling me that one of her roommates told her about a doctor who gives out pills that can make a woman miscarry. We got to talking about how many girls he might have gotten pregnant and if maybe others had taken the same pills. I have no idea how this would connect to the Pastor's untimely death, but still...." She let her monologue trail off.

I sighed in frustration. We already knew about the pill issue. Nothing new. Again.

"In case you didn't know," Mrs. Harker continued, despite my clearly audible sigh. "This doctor who has been helping girls end unwanted pregnancies is kind of a free pill dispensary. The pills are supposed to be for something else. I forget what, but anyway, they aren't legal. Not for ending a pregnancy."

"Do you know the doctor's name?" I asked hoping she would get the point and perhaps know something we didn't have yet so I could get back on the road and to work before Zack the Hack got into gear again and started pushing the wrong people around.

"Franks. Dr. Olivia Franks."

After thanking Jenny Harker for her call, I pulled back into traffic, eager now to get to my computer and do a little digging. Before I'd gone two blocks my phone buzzed again. This time I did glance at the caller-ID. Acosta.

"You on your way in, boss?"

Technically I wasn't his boss, but I didn't correct the young detective. "Almost there," I replied as I pulled onto U.S. 1. "What's up?"

"I did a little digging about that dentist you and Detective Oliver went to see the other day. The one you guys thought unlikely to offer anyone a threat?"

"And?" I prompted.

"And he was on the shooting team in college. He's an ace with a gun."

My heart jerked at the unexpected information. The meek, mild-mannered man in Smurf scrubs was a shooter? How had we missed that? Of course, there had been no awards or certificates adorning his office wall to give the fact away, but still… "We didn't find any guns registered to him when we looked," I countered.

"But his wife has some registered in her name. Her maiden name." Acosta sounded almost triumphant. "A whole bunch of them, in fact. She was on the same team in college. Probably where they met."

The wife! How had we not considered that possibility? A mother could be just as unforgiving as a father when her babies were threatened.

"Is Zack Oliver in yet?"

"He just walked by. Want me to fill him in?"

"No, just ask him to meet us in my office in twenty minutes. I'll be there in five. And I have one other thing for you to look up before I get there." I rattled off the pill doctor's name and the drug mentioned by Jenny Harker, then hung up and pulled out to pass the slower moving traffic in my way.

"She's a bit of an activist," Acosta said, meeting me at the door and following me as I hurried to my desk. "She doesn't agree with the current administration's stand on abortion and has been known to participate in protests, sometimes in Tallahassee. The drug mentioned is legal here for ulcers and I guess a few other things, but not for abortions. I couldn't find anything specific about her dispensing the stuff, but it fits with her political views. And she wouldn't have to go far to get a supply to just hand out under the radar."

I wasn't sure where this fit in yet, but it was information we needed to process. I cut the corner into my office, dropped my coat on the back of my chair and sat. "So, what else should I know about Merrick's wife before Oliver gets here?"

"Donna Hollister Merrick. She owns a dozen guns legally registered under Hollister. She's a member of Saltwaters Shooting Club and visits the Ancient City Range on a regular basis, too." Paul kept on firing facts at me like a tennis ball launcher as I booted up my computer to check a couple more things.

"You wanted to meet?" Zack appeared in my doorway.

I nodded toward the other vacant chair.

"Paul came up with some important information and I got a call from one of my informants with another angle to check out on the Price case."

Zack came in and sat without comment. Paul looked at me, eyebrows lifted to ask who should speak first.

"I think Paul has the most important bit of info, but first, maybe I should fill you in on my first call today."

Zack propped an ankle on his knee, with his usual, not expecting anything important, attitude.

I outlined the pills and abortion issue, and that at least one girl we'd been told about had taken the drug, then told her friends about how great it worked. Then I suggested the possibility that the dentist's daughter might have tried it with a less happy result. Then I gestured to Paul and let him take over.

As the results of Paul's digging were laid out, Zack's casual attitude began to desert him, until the foot hit the floor, his eyes flaring with newfound zeal.

"Where do we start?" Paul asked when his report was done.

Another thought suddenly hit me. "Dr. Franks might be the next victim. Maybe we need to start with her."

Zack cranked his head my way. "Franks?"

"If Merrick is our shooter, and if he went to the trouble of trying to get Ty tagged with the crime, revenge seems to be a likely reason to try to plant the murder weapon in his truck." I hoped I was making sense as my thoughts tumbled over each other.

"But they didn't put it in his truck," Paul objected.

"Only because whoever it was, got the wrong red truck," I said before Zack could add his opinion of Ty's innocence. "But if he tried to frame Ty, mightn't he seek retribution with the doctor who might have given his daughter the drugs in the first place?"

"We don't know that the doctor gave the girl drugs," Zack interrupted.

"No," I agreed. "We don't. But we don't know she didn't either. My informant seemed to think she did despite there being no cause of death listed in the obituary. The girl's father didn't mention any cause when we interviewed him either. Maybe he didn't think it mattered. Or maybe he was withholding information that he thought might incriminate him."

"We have nothing to tie the two together," Zack insisted.

"But nothing to discredit the possibility. Shouldn't we at least talk to the woman? Maybe we can rule her out and move on to the gun issue with the wife. But if she is involved, she might be in danger."

Zack was on his feet. "Okay. Let's get this over with."

Paul jumped to his feet as well, glancing from me to Zack, not sure of his role in the proceedings.

"We'll take two cars. You can ride with me." I pointed at Paul, grabbed my jacket, and headed for the door before Zack could suggest otherwise.

Halfway to the car, my phone buzzed again. This time it was my son. And he never called from school. I took the call.

"Mikey Mike. What's up?"

"You know that business you were telling Seth about the other night? About how Dr. Anderson wouldn't tell you who was yelling at him in his office?"

"Yeah?"

"Well, I know who it was. A friend of mine was waiting to see Dr. Anderson when it happened. She knows the guy because Dr. Merrick is her dentist. Does that help?"

"Mike, I love you. It's very helpful. Thanks for calling, but I can't chat right now."

"Me neither," Mike said clicking off before I could.

"Things are beginning to tie together," I told Paul as he fell into my passenger seat, pushing the laptop out of the way and pulling his door shut. "That was my son. And Merrick is the man who stormed Ty's office before all this went down.

"Humph!" Was Paul's reply.

"Buckle up," I told him, already pulling out so I could lead the way rather than eat Zack's dust.

CHAPTER 27

DR. FRANK'S OFFICE STOOD ALONE on a corner, a squat single-story building that might have been on the site for fifty years or could have popped up a year ago. Only three cars sat in the parking area, two in marked staff slots off to the right. Another lone car sat halfway down the side of the building on the left. It was early yet. Perhaps office hours didn't start until later and it was just staff currently in the building.

Zack straightened his jacket and glanced at the building before shrugging his shoulders at me. "How do you want to proceed?"

I told him about my son's call.

"Maybe we should get to Merrick first. Deal with this later if it still needs dealing with."

"But since we're here, we might as well warn her," I said heading for the front entrance.

"Are we going to discuss the illegality of the pills?"

"I'm not getting sucked into the abortion debate. We just need to find out enough to see if the doctor could be in danger, give her a heads-up maybe, and then get back to dealing with Merrick and his wife."

Zack nodded and followed me to the office door. Surprisingly, he pulled it open and held it for me to precede him.

A perky redhead looked up as we entered. "How may I help you?" She glanced at the three of us looming at the counter and her eager expression began to falter. "The office doesn't open until . . ."

"We just need a few moments of Dr. Franks' time," I said, glancing at the closed door behind the woman.

"She's—she's with someone at the moment." That explained the three cars in the lot.

"I though you said the office wasn't open yet?" Zack said stepping closer to the counter.

"Well, it's not. Not really. But a man came in saying he just needed a moment of time, too. Something about a counseling issue at school?" Suddenly alarmed, the woman got to her feet, glancing from the closed door to our trio and back. "What's going on?"

I whipped out my badge and Zack did the same. "Who is this other person?" Please God it was not the angry dentist.

"Dr. Merrick. I didn't think—" The woman looked to the closed door, back to our faces, then at the door again.

"Are there other doors besides that one?" I asked the scared looking woman.

"Th-that door leads to a hallway. There are three doors off that. One to Dr. Frank's personal office on the right. On the left is her consultation room. There's a back door to the parking lot at the end of the hall. Oh, and a bathroom."

If it had been Rafe with me, I wouldn't have had to say a thing. He'd have just moved into action. "You want to knock or go keep an eye on the rear door?" I asked.

"I'll go around back," Paul offered.

Before I had a chance to weigh the options Zack headed toward the closed door. I jerked my head for Paul to go around and joined Zack.

"Is there anyone else here besides you, Dr. Franks and Dr. Merrick?"

The frightened woman shook her head violently.

"Then I suggest you go sit in your car until we are done. Lock the doors."

She snatched her purse from the floor beside her chair and fled.

Zack rapped on the closed door but receiving no answer, pushed it open. The hallway was empty. The door to the consultation room stood open. It was empty.

Voices came from behind the closed door opposite.

"I am not responsible for your daughter's death." Presumably Dr. Franks. Her voice soft but clear.

"Those pills killed her." Dr. Merrick sounded nothing like the mild mannered children's dentist we'd spoken to just days ago.

"I assure you that medication is safe when used appropriately."

I desperately wished we could see through the solid wood of the door. Did Merrick have a gun trained on the woman, or was he just on another vocal rampage as he'd been when charging into Ty's office at the high school? There were always convenient keyholes in the doors of old fashioned who-dunnit movies. Not so here.

Zack raised his hand to rap on the door. I shook my head madly.

"What if he's got a gun?" I whispered.

Zack jerked his head. "You go left. I'll go right."

I slid my gun from its holster and nodded, then reached for the knob, praying it would not be locked.

I counted to three, then shoved the door open.

Two faces whipped around at our intrusion. The dentist, still clad in totally incongruous Smurf scrubs, looked even more shocked than Dr. Franks or her scared receptionist.

"What?" he croaked, looking like a cornered rat. But an armed, cornered rat. The most dangerous kind.

"I'll take that," Zack said, neatly stripping the dentist of his weapon.

I quickly holstered my gun and grabbed the man's free hand. I was in the process of snapping the cuffs on his wrists when another voice joined the fray.

"I might have known you'd screw it up." An unknown woman appeared behind Dr. Franks and wrapped an arm about her neck before either Zack or I could react. "Let him go or I shoot her."

That's when I belatedly noticed there was another door in this room, presumably a second entrance to the bathroom next door.

The woman, who would have been pretty with any other expression on her face, must be Donna Hollister Merrick. I released her husband but didn't remove the cuffs.

"And I'll take that, too." She nodded toward Zack and the gun he'd seized from Merrick.

"You were right, Donna," said Merrick, who had been speechless up to now.

The standoff continued. Merrick free but cuffed. Franks outwardly calm, but she had to be counting the minutes left in her life as Donna Merrick pulled a neat little Ruger LCR 22 from her pocket and pressed it against the doctor's temple. Zack still holding the larger gun Merrick had been waving in Dr. Franks direction when we entered. And me.

I had an awful feeling this was not going to end well. We should have checked the bathroom before assaulting the office where the confrontation was going on. My mistake. And it might cost us big.

Where was Paul?

"Put that gun on the floor and kick it my way," Donna Merrick demanded.

Zack carefully placed Dr. Merrick's gun on the floor by his foot but did not kick it her way as instructed.

"You don't hear too well, do you, smart ass?" Donna waved her little .22 toward Zack, her finger inside the trigger guard and on the trigger. "And while you're at it, I'll have your weapon, too. And yours." She let the gun barrel stray from Dr. Frank's head and aimed at Zack instead.

Crazy thoughts can run through your head at the worst possible times and right now I was pondering the pull pressure for that deadly little gun.

Before anything else could deter my thinking, Paul silently stepped up behind Donna Merrick.

Gun drawn, Paul had a finger to his lips. Unfortunately, Dr. Merrick saw him, too, and shouted a warning to his wife.

The next few moments of pandemonium had my heart rate in the red. Donna Merrick's gun went off, deafening in the confines of the office despite its diminutive size.

"Keeerist!" Zack cursed as he clapped a hand against the side of his head.

Donna Merrick slumped abruptly to the floor releasing Dr. Franks on her way down.

Paul's eyes went wide as he gazed at his pistol, then at the fallen woman.

Dr. Merrick dropped to his knees at his wife's side, pleading with her to answer him.

I had my gun out, ready for action but had nothing to shoot at.

CHAPTER 28

I GLANCED AT ZACK WHO CLUTCHED the side of his head, blood dripping between his fingers. The fact that he was cussing fluently gave me hope he wasn't seriously hurt as I hurried to the fallen woman's side to check her pulse.

She was alive, if less vocal, but I couldn't see where she'd been hit. I pulled Dr. Merrick away from his unconscious wife and jerked him to his feet.

"I didn't hit her that hard," Paul protested, gazing at the butt of his weapon. That explained the lack of a bullet wound.

"She'll live, then. Get a pair of cuffs on her and call 911 while I check on Zack." I took charge, trying to make order of the chaos.

Zack continued to curse, which I took as a good sign. He pulled his hand away from his head and winced. "I thought she was a crack shot."

"Either she was off her game, or you've got Paul to thank," I remarked pushing his hand back over the wound. "I'll find something to staunch the flow. Hang in there."

I dashed through the treacherous rear door and yanked a ream of paper towels from the dispenser, then hurried back to Zack's side. "Here." I pried his hand away from the wound and replaced it with the towels. "It's just a flesh wound but you're leaking like a severed fire hose."

"Stings like hell, too." He clutched the rapidly reddening towels to his head. He was going to have a whole new part to his hair. Maybe he'd have to start combing it to the other side for a while.

The wail of sirens was a welcome sound over the keening of Dr. Merrick. Moments later two uniformed deputies dashed into the room, followed by EMTs with heavy boxes of gear.

Donna Merrick was assessed by one of the medical team while Paul and the responding officers backed away to give them space. Merrick came to as she was strapped onto a backboard, and she began to thrash angrily.

"Just be still ma'am," the EMT soothed, pocketing his stethoscope, and rocking back on his heels. He glanced at me and rolled his eyes as the second uniformed officer urged Dr. Merrick to his feet.

The officer looked at me. "What'll I do with this one?"

"Take him to Central and book him for Price's murder—for starters."

"I should be with my wife," Dr. Merrick protested.

"Too bad." I had no sympathy for the man. I might have once felt sorry for the loss of his daughter, but his actions since my involvement in the case doused any softer emotions from me.

The deputy dragged Dr. Merrick from the room complaining loudly.

Dr. Franks had been assisted to a chair and looked to be in shock. Considering her office had been invaded by a madman, followed by said madman's wife holding a gun to her head, Franks probably *was* in shock. Someone would have to take her statement. And that of her receptionist.

"I'm not going in the ambulance," Zack insisted pugnaciously. "It's just a little blood."

"But sir," the EMT entreated, "You need to be looked at. It's going to require a few stitches at the very least."

"I'll take him," I offered. God, what brought that on? Last thing I needed right now was to ferry a reluctant fellow officer to the hospital. I turned to the two deputies who had responded and were standing around looking like they weren't sure what to do next. "You okay with taking Dr. Franks' statement and bagging the guns?"

"We got it, Ma'am," they responded in unison. That beat sitting out on U. S. 1 catching speeders.

"I'll ride back with Whelan," Paul volunteered. "Someone needs to make sure Merrick gets processed correctly. Besides, I've already got someone from internal wanting to interview me about taking Mrs. Merrick out, even if it was just a rap on the head. The sooner that's over, the happier I'll be." Then he smirked. "You can do the rest of the paperwork later."

I dug my keys out of my pocket. "Take my unit. I'll drive Zack's and collect mine later."

Paul had been key in getting this mystery solved, and he'd had our backs when we, the more experienced officers, had let our guard down. He deserved to crow a little.

By now there were a half dozen deputies milling around looking for something to make themselves look useful. Spying Deputy Anna Santos, I waved her over, and asked her to find the receptionist who might still be cowering in her car and take the woman's statement.

Just as I was climbing into the driver's seat of Zack's unit, I spotted Broussard headed our way. I straightened and waited.

"Where are you headed?" he asked slowing his energetic pace.

"Zack got a new part in his hair. I'm taking him to get it looked at."

"I heard he was giving the medic grief. Keep me posted. I'll wind things up here and see that Merrick gets booked."

"News travels fast," I said, wondering how he knew the details already. "We'll need a detail on Mrs. Merrick at the hospital, too. Until we're sure who fired the bullet that killed Price, she's a person of interest for that as well as holding a gun to Dr. Frank's head this morning."

"Acosta called me after he called 911. He filled me in on this morning's meeting, and the scene here while I was on my way over. So, it's over. And about time. Glad no one else got seriously injured." He ducked down to peer at Zack pouting in the passenger seat. He shook his head but made no comment before straightening again. "See you at Central." Then he turned and called out to another milling deputy and stalked that man's way.

The ER at Flagler was unusually quiet when Zack and I walked through the automatic doors and into the cool antiseptic interior.

Apparently, the desk staff had been alerted to our arrival. A young man in scrubs swung his hip around the end of the counter and signaled us to follow him.

"Zack's the one you want," I said giving my partner a nudge. "I'm just transport."

"But—" Zack started to protest.

"I'll wait out here." I pointed at the waiting nurse.

Just then the doors flew open, and another patient was wheeled through them, IV bag jiggling against a post affixed to the end of the gurney with an EMT rattling off details to the cluster of staff who rushed to meet them.

I found a quieter corner and slumped into a chair. I was tired. Surprisingly so. The results of adrenalin suddenly being shut down after it had been racing through my system to meet the demands of a tense situation. I slumped in the faux leather chair trying to decide which I needed more: Downtime or some caffeine.

Caffeine, I decided and dragged myself to my feet again.

I stood in front of the vending machine poking through my wallet for change when someone tapped my elbow.

"Our coffee's better." An older woman wearing volunteer garb who I'd seen before behind the intake desk held out a steaming ceramic mug.

"Bless you," I responded taking it from her and heading back to my corner.

I'd barely gotten settled when another group burst in, barely waiting for the automatic doors to finish opening before spilling into the waiting room. With a start, I recognized my daughter in their midst.

"Jacqui!" I exclaimed with alarm as I surged to my feet. What had brought her here in such a lather? Had something happened to Elliott? I hurried to my daughter's side.

"Mom!"

She fell on me, wrapping her arms around me, then dropping them almost as soon as the hug had begun. She stepped back and my heart fell. I'm not sure what I'd expected the next time I saw her after she'd abandoned my home in favor of her father's.

"Y-you're, okay?" Her eyes flew over me, down to my feet and back.

A willowy blond I vaguely recognized came up behind Jacqui. Elliott's girlfriend, I remembered with sudden clarity.

"Mom," Jacqui drew my attention back to her. "I thought . . . I thought it might be you that got shot."

"I tried to reassure her," the blonde, said. What was her name? My mind drew a blank.

"What made you think I'd been shot?" I asked, not only puzzled by her sudden appearance, but trying to fathom where she could have gotten such an idea.

"Mike. Or not exactly Mike, but he said you were investigating Dr. Franks. And then one of my friends said there was a shootout at Dr. Franks' office this morning and a detective got hit. And you wouldn't answer your phone, and Mike said he hadn't talked to you since first period, and Daddy didn't know anything and—" Her words, tumbled over each other making less sense as they went, until she finally stopped talking and threw her arms around me again.

Her body shook with sobs I was still trying to comprehend. I held her, rocking her as I'd done when she was still small enough to sit on my lap, until they finally stopped.

"I love you, Mom," she whispered wetly into my neck.

"Love you too, Punkin," I replied using the pet name she'd scorned so recently.

Finally, she pulled herself together and let go. "Is Rafe going to be okay?"

I took her hand and drew her toward my still relatively deserted corner and my now cold mug of coffee. "Rafe is on leave. I've been working with two other detectives on this case. Detective Oliver received a shallow head wound, but you know how head wounds bleed. I brought him in to get it cleaned out and stitched up."

"I feel like such a fool," Jacqui said, then pressed her lips together.

"Don't. The fact that you cared and came running makes me feel good inside." Suddenly all the dissonance of the last few months, and her defection to Elliott's house melted away and I caught a glimpse of a new, more adult relationship between us.

Maybe it was a good thing I didn't have to be chief disciplinarian and caretaker now. Instead, we could explore a relationship that included friendship and shared time doing things together we both enjoyed. Like shopping for clothes. And laying on the beach in the dark counting stars.

Jacqui twisted her hands in her lap, biting her lips. Her brain busy with thoughts I couldn't guess at. She glanced up at Brandy Lovejoy. The name came to me like a slap. Whatever passed between Miss Lovejoy and my daughter had Miss Lovejoy shrugging her shoulders and drifting off toward the other side of the waiting area. Clearly, they enjoyed some kind of communication I did not, but before I could let that begin to sink in and fester, Jacqui grabbed my hand.

"I'm sorry about that awful boy I let come up to my room, and I'm sorry about how I treated you. I don't know what I was thinking. Mike told me he was bad news. But I didn't want to listen. Anyway. He's history. I just want us to be friends again." This was said with a hint of doubt, maybe tinged with regret. As an apology, it was more than I'd imagined I'd ever get. And maybe more than I deserved.

Our falling out as mother and daughter was as much my fault as hers. I'd been so focused on my career within the sheriff's department, I'd missed all the clues that I should have seen in her discontent.

I pulled her into an embrace. Time for a reset. "I'm sorry, too, Punkin."

"Mo-om!"

Okay. Now we were back to normal. Or our new normal. My heart felt lighter than it had in months. "Jacqueline," I corrected myself.

"Can we go shopping this weekend? I have nothing to wear."

Laughing, I agreed.

My daughter then launched into a detailed recital of everything that had happened in her life since the morning I'd told her she could move to Elliot's house. I eased us back to my cooling mug of coffee, and we sat as she went on, and I sipped.

Finally, she ran out of events and glanced over to where Miss Lovejoy patiently waited in front of a television showing a re-run of the Golden Girls.

"I guess I should get going. I still have homework to finish." Jacqui stood up.

"Call me, and we'll plan a whole day of shopping," I told my daughter as I got to my feet, and hugged her one more time before watching her cross the room to the woman who'd brought her to my side with no questions asked. It was going to take some adjusting. Maybe a lot of adjusting. But things were looking happier already.

Zack, being pushed in a wheelchair, appeared just moments after my daughter followed her ride out the revolving door into the mid-afternoon sunshine. His head was swathed in white, and his face was almost as pale as the dressings.

"Time to take the walking wounded home where he belongs?"

Zack grimaced. "I'd rather be headed to Central."

"No, you don't. You're just saying that, but you really need to give yourself a little time to recover."

"I'll wheel him out when you bring up the car," the orderly suggested as he put a hand on Zack's shoulder to ease him back into the wheelchair.

CHAPTER 29

THE REMAINDER OF THE WEEK SEEMED to fly by one moment, then dragged to the pace of a funeral procession the next.

The paperwork fallout had been expected, along with all the interviews, both internal relating to the shooting and to Paul Acosta's having taken out Donna Merrick by striking her with the butt of his gun. No charges were ever brought regarding the graffiti, and Paul had acquired an informant of his own in Dusty, who, by way of his visits to St Francis House, seemed to know far more of what went on in the darker side of St Augustine than I did.

I was able to get away long enough to attend Rafe's dad's funeral and give my partner a long overdue hug. I assured him I'd welcome him back however long he was gone even if Zack and I had managed to come to a place where we could work together without constant sniping.

The Anderson's lives began to return to their new normal now that Ty was no longer in Zack's crosshairs. Kiara had landed safely back in the big city. Keisha was back to her usual at school and their oldest son had departed with his family. I'd even seen Natalie sitting under their aged oak tree painting a picture of their solder son from memory. There would always be a hole where their son had been, but that too would begin to hurt less as time went on.

Ty's dad had begun to settle into his new digs, and Mike had volunteered to take him grocery shopping for things Natalie would never have approved, but the older man craved. An unlikely friendship seemed to have blossomed between the two, and the next outing had been a ride along A1A in Mike's refurbished Camaro. Mr. Anderson insisted it was the best day ever. I was proud of my son for reaching out to an old, and often confused, new neighbor, helping him find peace and enjoyment in his new situation.

I had returned to my spare time investigation into Sam Cameron's disappearance, but to date, had not learned anything new. I'd contacted the original investigating officer who was now retired, but he'd promised to send me copies of his notes, some of which had not made it into the official file. I wasn't giving up. Seth had carried that crusade all his life and I was determined to stay with it.

And today, Jacqui and I'd been on our promised shopping spree. I stood in my bedroom, bags of all shades and sizes strewn across my bed. Jacqui and I had a marvelous time, laughing and closer than we'd been in months. I spent way more than I should have on clothes I'd rarely get to wear, but it had been fun. More fun than we'd shared in a long time. And it was only money, after all.

I started pulling things from the bags and hunting through my closet for hangers. Seth was coming over for dinner and I needed to decide which new outfit I'd wear.

The winning choice was the maroon mini-skirt Jacqui insisted I needed. I'd thought it was too short, but she thought it flattered my legs. To go with it, I chose a soft off-white cashmere top that dipped low to reveal more of my cleavage than I was used to. Wearing suits and slacks to work, and shorts and t-shirts to the beach had gotten me well away from wearing anything even remotely sexy.

By the time I finished with my makeup and hair, I could hear men's voices in the kitchen. Barely recognizing the woman in the mirror, I sucked in a heartening breath and headed for the kitchen.

Mike, holding a tray of shucked corn, was headed for the barbeque on the deck when I stepped into view. He glanced at me, eyes widening, then at Seth. Then Mike grinned, winked at me, and headed outside.

Seth's reaction was equally rewarding. '*Thank you, Jacqui,*' flitted through my head.

"You look . . ." Seth began and trailed off.

"Overdressed for a barbeque at home?" I offered.

"So sexy," he growled. "And perfect for a barbeque at home."

Supper was fun and filled with great conversation. I enjoyed listening to Mike and Seth debate the high school football team's chances of turning a several-year losing streak around. Then the discussion moved on to college ball and the teams fielded by the two university choices Mike waffled between for his college career. I was just happy to relax, be waited on by my son who was becoming quite the cook and having my wine glass kept filled by a man who clearly admired me as a woman.

Eventually Mike took himself to his room and Seth and I drifted out to the deck to admire the moon rising over the ocean.

"Is Zack still behaving?" Seth asked, turning his back on the romantic scene unfolding to the east.

"Tonight, it's just us," I said pressing a finger against his lips.

He kissed my finger, then pulled me toward him. "In that case," he murmured, lowering his forehead to mine. "Have I told you how fabulous you look?"

"I think you did. A few times." My heart raced at the heat filling his gaze.

He kissed me then. Gently. Seeking what, I wasn't sure. But there was no doubt in my mind about what I wanted. I leaned in until my body molded to his, then parted my lips.

His hands hovered only briefly at my back before sliding down to cup my buttocks, pulling me and all my soft parts against all his hard ones.

The kiss deepened and I lost all sense of time and place. Seth's mouth devoured mine, awaking a passion I'd done my best to ignore for too long. I pulled the tails of his shirt out of his waistband and slid my palms across the warm bare skin of his back. I wanted this man more than I'd wanted anything in a long time.

Into my head came the image of us in my bedroom, shutting the door and tearing each other's clothes off as we stumbled to the bed, breathing hard and kissing harder.

And suddenly, it was like someone had dumped a bucket of cold water over me. I stiffened and pulled away. Pulled my hands out from under his shirt and placed them flat against his chest. I glanced over my shoulder at the empty living room beyond. "This can't happen."

Seth didn't fight me. He didn't even groan in disappointment. He just gazed down at me with a frown creasing his forehead. He swallowed hard and his Adam's apple bobbed.

"I'm sorry."

"No!" The denial burst from my mouth. "You've nothing to be sorry about. It's just . . . just . . ."

He leaned forward and rested his forehead against mine again. He was still breathing hard, but his hands now rested on my shoulders without a hint of the powerful desire he'd been consumed by just moments before.

"Just what? You don't want me as much as I want you?"

I shook my head. I probably wanted him more than he wanted me, considering the thoughts that had ravaged my self-control just moments before. But that vision of us, in my bedroom, had triggered a memory of me chastising my daughter for having a boy in her bedroom just a few months earlier.

Sure, I was an adult, and she was just barely into her teens, but it still struck me as two-faced. A double standard I'd have a hard time defending. Mike wouldn't see any problem with me sleeping with Seth, but I'd feel awkward having Seth show up in the kitchen, tousled from sleep, while Mike was slurping down a bowl of cereal.

"Just not yet?" he whispered.

"Just not here," I finally managed to explain. Not that it was much of an explanation, but immediately, he seemed to get it.

He lifted his hands from my shoulders to cup my face. This kiss was deep yet gentle. Nothing of the earlier passion, but a world of caring. Then his mouth turned up in a half-smile.

"I'll let myself out and we can talk about this later. When we've both had time to think about what we want to happen next. And . . ." He bobbed his head side to side. "And how we plan to explain it to our kids."

If you enjoyed this book, please consider leaving a review on Goodreads or wherever you purchased this book.

Acknowledgments

Striking out into an entirely new genre was made possible by so many helpful people. I couldn't have done it without you.

There were two wonderful deputies with my local sheriff's department who allowed me to go for a ride-along. Thanks to Tony Clark and Nicole Burrell and her K-9 Ryker, for taking responsibility for my safety and showing me what a patrol officer's job is really like. Thanks also to the entire staff of The Citizens Law Enforcement Academy who shared their knowledge and experiences in classes covering all aspects of police work, including a few four-footed deputies. And a very special thanks to Sgt. Samantha James who generously answered my many questions about working on the Major Crimes Squad.

Thanks also to my Sandy Scribbler writing buddies for their ongoing encouragement, and excellent brainstorming sessions. And to the lovely lady, who wishes to remain nameless, who spent valuable time copy editing and critiquing my work.

Skye Taylor, mother, grandmother and returned Peace Corps Volunteer, lives in St Augustine Florida where she enjoys the history of America's oldest city and daily walks on its beautiful beaches with her pooch, Jessi. She is currently working on a whole new series set on Bailey Island Maine where she vacations every summer. Her published work includes: *Bullseye*, *The Candidate*, *Falling for Zoe*, *Loving Meg*, *Trusting Will*, *Healing a Hero*, *Keeping His Promise*, *Worry Stone*, *Believing in Mac, and Iain's Plaid*. Visit her website: www.Skye-writer.com to read some of her short stories and her essays about her time spent in the South Pacific with the Peace Corps. She is a member of Sisters in Crime, Florida Writer's Association, and Women's Fiction Writers Association. She loves hearing from her readers at Skye@Skye-writer.com